<u>JUDGE</u>

By

Brandon W. Neumann

JUDGE

ISBN: 9781717713391

Table of Contents

Thank you all for your support

You may now enjoy this book…

~ CHAPTER 1 ~

THE TOWN

Peter was 12. After walking around the quieter parts of the Town for some time, he found a bench in an area that had many trees and people that blew around the walking paths like the leaves of the trees. He had become fascinated with observing this natural steady flow of what he had learned to perceive as life. He spent about ten minutes doing this until pulling out his book about birds of prey. He stared intensely at the picture of the peregrine falcon. Wondering about the meaning of "peregrine," he excitedly recalled his pocket dictionary, which he carried around so as to boost his vocabulary to better express himself; reaching for it in his backpack, he looked up the definition. It read,

> "peregrine
>
> (per-i-grin)
>
> 1. foreign; alien; coming from abroad.
>
> 2. wandering, traveling, or migrating."

Peter quite liked that; indeed he even played with the idea of somehow changing his name to that: Peregrine Fischer. He slowly drifted off into daydreaming about flying. He wandered back to the picture of the bird, the mountain catching his attention, wondering where this mountain was, he resolved that tomorrow he would go climb a mountain since it had been a long while since he had gone hiking. He felt he deserved it. In the midst of all this, Peter Peregrine Fischer along with the other leaf people suddenly heard an unmistakable, yet nevertheless shocking still, sound of a gunshot. Due to the common occurrence of these types of events in this particular Town, the people continue on their routines. It seemed as though they still had a certain fear about them—a fear to acknowledge what had happened, a fear to accept, or to face it. Although their faces remained expressionless, you could see it in their eyes.

Peter, however, was perturbed. Of course, he had heard almost daily about vile and lesser crimes, which, by now, seemed unworthy to be deemed crimes but rather "just the flaws of the society," as the people saw it. He wondered what was the cause? What on this big blue earth would compel a man or woman to act that way? Peter was different. Peter was curious. He packed up his books as well as his thoughts and started walking home. Slightly out of fear to get away from the scene, but mainly out of anxiety to think it out on the way.

Peter had a very musical walk; he possessed a sort of rhythm in his steps, with the thoughts flying through his head as the lyrics to the song, which was composed as he walked. The song seemed to always fit the mood—this time it was a somber tune. This particular supposed murder or attack by gun had struck Peter more than the other inconceivable acts. Staring at the sidewalk intently as if the answers were written there, reading the reasons behind the act, he tried to find a conclusion, an answer. Peter, though, was too young and inexperienced to finalize this dilemma. So, for now this quandary would stay with him, as if to be packed away in his backpack along with the others and his books. He found at least *some* comfortable answer that worked for him for this point in time.

As he lifted his eyes upward, there were plenty of birds for him to observe and identify and keep him occupied. This took his mind off of the problem at hand. His thoughts on the subject flew away with the birds. A grin returned to Peter's face. After all, it was still a good day.

Continuing on the homeward path, after spotting several blue jays, hummingbirds, sparrows and robins, something new caught his eye. On the opposite side of the street, sitting calmly was a dog. This dog was a beautiful whitish-cream color, elegantly poised without a collar. They glanced at each other, locking eyes for a moment, and in that moment there was a feeling of both familiarity and contentment. Among the garbage and deterioration of the Town—the lowlifes and the filth of the streets—this dog along with the blue jays and hummingbirds and the occasional squirrel gave him something to direct his attention away from the decay.

On the streets, one hears many unpleasant and unwelcomed noises. The shrill cries and complaints of a society gone under, or rather divided asunder; the sounds of breaking glass, rampant yelling, the distant screams of victims of assault, theft, vandalism, kidnapping; you name it, they've got it. Of course, not everyone in the Town is as unfortunate as these souls; indeed, it had seemed like this place was overrun with a decrepitude, but that is only because of the vividness or prevalence of these scenes in the everyday life. Many a happy family and individual (although, some refrain from defining it as "happiness," since both groups *claim* to be happy) live amongst it in fact, only in the right part of town, such as where Peter lives. Peter wanted that, which he could not find in the places where he searched; he has long wanted to escape, to break away, hence the frequent bird watching. Peter is easily persuaded, and this Town is quite a melting pot of different views and ideals; all of which are very enticing to the young boy. Oftentimes he doesn't know where to turn; on which of the paths laid before him by those who have more experience with life than him he should go. So, he looks to the birds, the animals, and the mountains, concurrently, however, still frequenting the streets of the Town. He seeks balance, or perhaps justice.

Andrew, Peter's good friend, spotted him walking a while back and catching up to him he called out, "Hey, Pete! What's up?"

"Hey, Andy, not much. Hey, did you hear that gunshot?" Peter replies with a sense of concern in his voice.

"Which one?" Andy answered sarcastically. "You alright? Why're you so worried about it? It happens all the time! Anyways, you wanna see what I got?"

"Sure, what is it?" answers Peter dissatisfied.

Andy looks around suspiciously as he pulls an attractive watch out of his pocket.

Peter, shocked, hurriedly tries to hide it and force him to shove it back in his pocket, "Where did you get that?" he blurts.

"Relax! I found it on the ground next to some trashcans. I'm not a thief if that's what you're thinking, and look! It's in almost perfect condition!" says Andy excitedly.

"Dude, that's cool and all but you're gonna get us—" Right then, suddenly they heard a loud noise come from around the corner that startled them into a sprint in the opposite direction. Andy nonchalantly chuckled with a smug look on his face, as if running and tempting the loss of his innocence gave him an insatiable thrill. Outwardly, Andy had no fear; but everyone has fear, however people may try to cover it or deny it, it lurks nevertheless. Inwardly, Peter held an envy of his supposed fearlessness because of his own immense display of outward fearfulness.

Peter and Andy's sprint dissolved into a steady quickened pace until it settled as normal walking. Peter, with an annoyed laugh says, "I've gotta go, man, I'll see you later."

Andy with the same smugness replies, "Alright, buddy, take it easy!"

They split paths and Peter continues on his subconsciously memorized trail towards home, walking past the "funky-looking apple tree," then past the house with the purple mailbox and matching door, turning the corner at the fire hydrant, finally, after the house with the long driveway leading to a garage door that is always half-open, approaching the long fence with the barking dog, he is welcomed home by the smell of the dinner that always awaits his arrival. These scenes become the backdrop to his final thoughts. Peter settles in and mentally plans out his hike for tomorrow.

The Town in which Peter lives holds a wall of striking mountains—a stark contrast to the vileness of the streets—with a broad selection of hiking trails from which to choose. Peter goes to the mountain for the mountain and what it has to offer, so he usually picks either the least populated trails or not a trail at all. With the mountains not far from home, Peter takes off the next morning with nothing but his iPod and some water. As he approaches the trailheads, he finds a particularly attractive giant rock a ways up the slope, atop which he will climb to sit and think. On the way up he spots three deer, and stops to watch them as they graze in such a serene manner. He finds it ironic, because typically when you encounter deer, they are frantic and petrified, ruthlessly struggling to escape a speeding car or shot of a rifle. When in reality, despite the fact that all *we* see of deer is a scene of that struggling, they likely live a majority of their life grazing and migrating peacefully from one meadow to the next. A smile eases gradually onto his face like a glass being filled with water.

Perched atop his stone watchtower, Peter looks out on the Town and lets the sensations soothe his troubled soul. He has wisdom beyond his years. He observes. He ponders. Though, as a result of his years, he remains troubled because he finds either insubstantial or no answers at all, but he shirks it off. He goes with the flow, not worrying much. Of course, his thoughts don't always encircle these cares. He is still just a kid—his mind practically entertains itself; he thinks about the music to which he listens, wishing he could play the drums or guitar, about what he will eat when he gets home, about his dreams, about how he can't wait for the snow, about who invented the vacuum and on and on, continuing in a cyclical process.

After drinking his fill out of the punch bowl of his thoughts, one of his favorite songs cues the descent of the mountain. On his way down, he stops to be entertained by two squirrels having a stare down, which then begin to fight and chase each other around the rocks and up a tree; this humors Peter, releasing some much needed laughter. He is fine and composed on the mountain, but the sun begins to set, and as he hits the outskirts and inner parts of the Town, his pace is quickened and eyes widened. He removes one of his headphones for caution sake.

Suddenly, Andy stumbles out from around the corner with his head down, startling Peter. "Andy, what are you doing out here? You scared me!" he exclaims.

"Oh, hey Pete. Nothin'. I'm just walkin' around," he says.

Peter notices how he's keeping his head down and hidden, with his hands in his pockets and hood from his jacket on, as if out of shame. "What's wrong?" he asks. After receiving only the shuffling of feet as an answer from Andy, Peter repeats the question. Still getting nothing, he asks, "Is it your dad again?"

Andy sniffles.

"Come on, man!" Peter pries.

"It was that watch, okay?" he quickly replies with frustration and embarrassment.

Peter notices he has a black eye. "Dude. I'm sorry," he says. "Let's get out of here."

Andy submits, not showing his gratitude for Peter's consolation. They begin walking together.

"I'm sick of this place," says Andy, "I just don't know what to do."

"I've heard it's like this in other towns outside of here though. So, I don't know if there is anything you *can* do."

Andy sighs, then spews, "Why does it have to be like this?"

Peter remains quiet.

They walk in the silence of yearning and contemplation for several more steps. They come upon an empty street to the right, empty, that is, except that it was concealing a car that is visibly older but still intact excluding one broken window,

"Let's go check it out!" says Andy, with a tone of gladness from this distraction.

Peter, torn between curiosity and knowledge of boundaries not to be crossed, succumbs and joins him. Having second thoughts the whole time, trying to convince Andy to stop and just leave, Peter couldn't help but wonder what Andy planned on doing or what they would find. As they approached the car, a rank stench emanated therefrom, Peter remained a reasonable distance away from the car while Andy scoured the inside of the car through the windows, his curiosity and determination to make this detour worthwhile trumping the smell. "Andy, come on, let's get outta here, it stinks, and we don't know whose that is, they could come back any second!" says Peter as he frantically looks around cautiously.

Andy ignores Peter, and then exclaims, "Dude! There's 20 bucks in here!" with a tone of success.

"Serious?" said Peter with a peaked curiosity, stepping a little closer, "You're not really gonna take it, are you? What if you get caught?"

A prideful Andy replies, "Calm down, man. This thing has been abandoned for a while now, *and* I'm 20 dollars richer than I was 20 dollars ago!"

"How do you know that?" retorts Peter, ignoring Andy's wit.

Andy freezes.

At this moment, Peter is startled by a dog, which he spots in the corner of his eye, that walks by glancing at Peter and continues on, Peter looks back at Andy, who had spotted the watch that he found from earlier, lying in the car.

"Alright, let's go" he says abruptly.

Peter didn't ask questions, as he was glad to leave. After a few minutes of walking, Peter asks with a smirk on his face, "So, what are you going to buy with the 20 dollars?"

Andy laughs.

This Town's layout includes an outer guardian wall of sorts, made of mountainous legions, which protect the concourses of homes, mansions, apartment complexes, office buildings, and the people who inhabit them. The center of Town is the most heavily populated, and it seems like more and more people choose to be closer to the center of Town and they move in, and vice versa, a number of people (smaller than the opposing) choose to be closer to the mountains, further from the chaos of the Town center, and they move to the outskirts. As the sun's light and the blackness of night trade shifts over the Town, there appears to remain a separate but very *real* form of lightness and darkness looming over the Town. The densely packed center of Town is occupied by the darkness, while in the outskirts the blackness is vacated and replaced by the lightness. On the mountainside, visible from almost anywhere in the Town, sits a great white mansion, and it is rumored that the wealthiest man lives there, alone. They say that he either owns most of the property and buildings in the Town, or he owns the *entire* Town; some say that he helped build it. Most of the people have had a run-in with him in one way or another, and less people know him well and revere him. He has been around a long time, and so has the Town.

The people of the Town are quite mundane, whether in the center or the outskirts. The segregation doesn't seem to cause too many prevailing disputations; although contentions *do* arise between the two sides, if you could call them by that term; mostly, unless certain errands need to be run, the people generally keep to themselves. There doesn't seem to be much that drives these people. Perhaps for this very reason the segregation exists—it takes very little for these people to be persuaded to choose that, which they will allow to be their *essence*; they choose the lifestyle, which they believe will bring them happiness, and it's different for everyone. In Peter's comings and goings of the outskirts and the center, there are a few apparent differences between the two crowds of people, but just in passing it isn't easy to recognize the distinction between one who lives in the center versus a resident of the outskirts. One has to spend an adequate amount of time with either one, until it becomes clear.

~ CHAPTER 2 ~

THE NEW FRIEND

Peter is now 15 years old. He arrived at the bench where he would come and watch the people walk to and from the next destinations of their ritualistic lives. Peter recognized many faces; and some days that would include the face of the girl he saw about a week and a half ago, a girl that was so beautiful that she hooked him and reeled him in, and she was completely unaware of it. He sits on an empty bench—empty except for his backpack and the hope that he will find her and she will notice him—waiting and searching relentlessly the passing faces for her. This has become *his* ritualistic life as of late; he was no stalker though, of course. As his discouragement and frustration grows, he began to pack up to leave when Ketten came and sat to join him at the bench. "I suppose you're happy that I didn't find her today aren't you?" Peter says. A few moments of silence compel their departure.

"Where are we going today, Ketten?" asks Peter. Still no answer, as he leads him down the street away from

the park. "Look, I've gotta know, dude. I've got plans."
Ketten glances back at him. Peter submits for a while
longer. Curiosity is what kept Peter tethered to Ketten, that
and the lack of companionship otherwise. At first it is a
pleasant stroll that began at the park, passing the nicer
buildings, workplaces and small office buildings of the
people of the Town. Peter's skepticism was distracted by
this panorama. The familiarity of the display of scenery
and architecture began to fade, and his skepticism
transformed gradually into a trance-like shadowing of
Ketten along with a belief that he was leading him
somewhere of value as they progressively wandered
further in strange roads. He concealed his hope that it
might have had something to do with the nameless girl for
which he has been waiting, or that maybe he would run
into her.

An airplane overhead snaps Peter out of his
trance-like state; he is now captured by the long billowy
contrails, and daydreams that he is a passenger, heading to
the unknown destination, temporarily detached from the
ground, bound to the sky. Not knowing where he currently
was, he declared to Ketten, "Alright, it's time to go home,
I'll see you later." Ketten whined. "Sorry, dude, I told you
I had plans." Peter starts off on his way home, taking

whichever streets looked like they led eventually to the center of Town or someplace recognizable. A disappointed Ketten stares him down, as he gets further away, until finally he is consumed by the next alleyway.

On his way, Peter was accompanied by feelings of puzzlement, insecurity, and discomfort. He let them run their course as he subconsciously trailed homeward. Wishing he had had his music with him, he couldn't wait to get home to play on his guitar, as he had planned, for hope that it would be an antidote to these negative feelings. He didn't know why he was feeling this way, he didn't think that he did anything wrong, or even questionable.

Peter began to recall his first encounters with Ketten from over two years ago. His 13th birthday was approaching and he was getting excited because that year he had asked for a guitar and his hopes were high. It was also a time of the year when he was feeling very alienated, isolated and lonely. Even though he was not particularly *alone*, loneliness was present. Peter, from the outside, wasn't an evidently depressed boy, he laughed a lot (mostly at himself and his own jokes) and had a lot of fun, but he did have a lot of internal battles. Peter did not know the root cause of this loneliness or any of his depressiveness; all he knew was that he had these feelings.

One day Peter and Andy were playing basketball on an open court near the park. Peter had a littler body type than Andy but was quicker on his feet and very nimble. Neither of them was any sort of athlete, but they enjoyed playing for fun, for recreation. Peter had just scored a point to teeter the score in his favor when their cheering and banter was at once robbed by the sight of three older thuggish boys approaching them.

Andy was a punk, believing he was bigger than he actually was, "Oh, you guys wanna play some basketball?" he yelled sarcastically. That was the spark that ignited the flame; they started to sprint towards the young pair obviously catalyzing their escape. "Let's split up!" yelled Andy. Peter veered left and Andy darted to the right. The older boys split up too, two of them going after Andy and one chasing Peter. Peter, sprinting vigorously, didn't look back. The older boy gets close enough to grab his arm, Peter yanks it away, but the boy latches on again, pulling him down to the ground. Peter tries to wriggle out of his clutches, but is unsuccessful. "Get off me! What do you want?" he yells. The boy pins him down and punches him three times in the face. Then, just as quickly as they came, the boy got up and ran off leaving a bloodied, battered and broken Peter. This type of behavior resembles that of some amateur gang-like group initiation.

Peter, still lying on the ground, began to weep. These are tears brought on by the pain, confusion, and lonesomeness. Once Peter had had enough of soaking in his own blood and tears, he pulled himself together and got up off the ground. Still in utter disarray, he looked around to try and figure out where he was and to where Andy might have run. He wondered if he got caught too, and if he was okay. "Andy!" he called out loud enough to be heard, but quietly for fear of the thugs returning. "Andy, where are you?" he called out again after hearing no reply. He couldn't have gotten far from where he was Peter thought. Mainly, Peter's focus was to get out of there, to somewhere safe, but he was still concerned for his friend. He looked down a few more streets, calling out with each searching glance, before moving onwards towards home. Crying some more tears, and in wonderment as to why this happened, Peter was stopped in his tracks and met by something in his peripherals. Tears quenched and breath held he slowly looks to the left. The figure that had been stalking him crept out of the shadows. There stood a dog.

Peter sighed with relief and smiled. Then he realized that he recognized this dog, he had seen it before. He remembered it because it was a rather peculiar-looking dog. It had pointed ears, and its fur was a mix of many dark colors, with a blackened snout and paws. It was no bigger than a standard, adult Labrador (although, that was not the breed of the dog). Around its neck, it wore a chain collar with a dangling tag. There was a strange attraction to this dog; Peter felt a pulling curiosity drawing him in. Peter had seen this dog for the first time when he and Andy were searching through the car with the broken window; it was the same dog that startled him. The dog didn't seem to behave like a typical dog and for this reason Peter was a little tentative at the sight of him. The dog just stood there staring at him, breathing heavily with its tongue hanging out as if he had been running. Peter, taking his chances with trusting him, called out, "come here!" patting his hands on his thighs. The dog perked its ears up, tilted its head, and closed its mouth. "Why you bein' so mysterious?" Peter uttered under his breath with a sense of hesitation. At that moment, the dog came over with his ears down and his head tucked down. He came right up to Peter's feet. Peter, a bit frightened and surprised, crouched down and reached out to pet him. The dog seemed to accept the scratching behind the ears with joy and gratitude. "You're just a nice fella aren't you?" said Peter now letting his guard down.

Peter stood up and the dog immediately jumped up on him licking his tears and the blood from the wounds on his face. "Hey!" Peter shouted with laughter. The dog jumped down and looked up at him. Peter felt comforted by this dog's visit. For a moment, he had forgotten about the incident. He suddenly noticed the dangling tag from his collar; he stooped down to see what it read: "Ketten." "'Ketten,' is that your name?" Peter asked the dog. "Well, Ketten, it was nice to meet you, thanks for the visit, but I have to get home now. I hope to see you again." He gave him a couple more pats on the head before departing. Ketten just started following him. Peter, bewildered by his sudden companionship, scolded the dog, "Hey, I gotta go now, you can't come with me, they wouldn't like it too much back at home. So, stay!" As he turned to leave again, he noticed Ketten was following him again. "Look, buddy, I told you, you can't come with me. Stay!" he showed him the palm of his hand, "stay," he repeated. Ketten sat down. Peter smiled, "alright, good boy. Bye!" Peter regained his focus and traveled home. Peter's path home was led by a mind with an overwhelming accompaniment of blaring emotions leftover from the preceding twenty minutes or so of events. He felt a very strange and unsettling feeling, he felt *uneasy*. He couldn't stop thinking about that dog, nor about whether or not Andy was okay.

A few days had passed by, and although Peter had not made it outside much since the incident, he still hadn't seen or heard from Andy. The worrying had settled though by this point and Peter presumed that this meant Andy was fine. Not three weeks later, Peter's birthday had finally come. Peter's excitement at the top of the morning was flowing over the brim; the anticipation was making him itchy and agitated. He was feeling good, receiving many birthday wishes from some friends and relatives. Towards the end of the day, he had received what appeared to be all of the gifts. He didn't think that that was it; he hoped he was going to be surprised with one last gift—the guitar, for which he'd been pestering and hinting at for some time now. When the realization set in that he would evidently not be gifted a guitar, his hope dwindled and converted to depression. He started to wonder if anyone actually listened to or cared about him at all. Peter left the house sulking and went to wander the streets to clear his head and get his mind off of this letdown.

Peter got himself to the heart of the Town, but what surrounded him didn't seem to faze him. He just walked with his head hung down; hands in his pockets, passing multiple scenes that would ordinarily be cause for trepidation. Then, unexpectedly, he felt a nudge on his leg from the snout of a dog—Ketten. "Hey, Ketten." he greeted him bleakly. Ketten walked by his side. Peter didn't know if he was happy to see him or if it would just make things worse. Since Peter was already wandering aimlessly, he just followed Ketten's lead. "It's my birthday today, ya know," he stated, hopeful of recognition. Ketten was a dog, therefore did not respond or acknowledge Peter's plea for attention. "I didn't even get the guitar I asked for. Don't they know that I wanted that more than anything? That would make me happier than any *other* gift!" he expressed to Ketten with frustration, "You would have given me a guitar wouldn't you?" he joked.

Right at this moment, a familiar voice caught Peter off guard, "Who you talkin' to?" said Andy.

Peter gasped with surprise and excitement to see his friend, "Andy! I was just talking to Kett—," he pointed to his side, only to see that the dog had disappeared, "oh, I guess he left. How are you? What happened to you?" he said, noticing that Andy had not a single bruise or cut.

"I got away, man. I hid and they couldn't even find me. It looks like they got you though huh? I'm sorry, dude! I stayed hidden for a while after, and I just assumed you got away too." confessed Andy, slightly ashamed for having not been beaten up.

"You got away! Well, thanks for helping *me* out!"

"Well, what did you want me to do?" said Andy with an irritated tone.

Peter was silent for a moment, until recognizing it wasn't Andy's fault that he was attacked. "So, do you know who those guys were?" he asked.

"Nah, man, no idea." answered Andy. They started walking somewhere else, not knowing where they'd end up. "Oh! I almost forgot, happy birthday, you stupid nerd!" he said to lighten the mood, and tossed him a small wrapped present.

Peter laughed and thanked him; "Thanks, chump!" and he opened the gift. The torn newspaper revealed a small stuffed panda. He laughed, "Oh wow! My life is now complete, I have everything I've ever wanted!" he remarked sarcastically.

"I found it! And I thought you might like it. Sorry it looks like he soiled himself. There also may or may not be something inside it," Andy smirked.

"Oh boy!" he exclaimed, then peered inside the hole, moving the stuffing around to find a 5-dollar bill. "You didn't have to do that, man. Thanks, buddy," he said gratefully.

"Well, actually I gave you that so both of us could go share it and get some tacos," he said smugly.

"You dirty dog!" Peter chuckled, "Come on, let's go."

Later when they were sitting eating tacos, Peter asked Andy, "So do you remember that night when we found that old car that you went looking through?"

Andy, puzzled, answered, "Yeah, what about it?"

Peter stalled for a moment, "Did you see that dog that was off to the side?"

"No, I don't know *what* you're talking about, dude, why?" replied Andy somewhat twitchy to hide his sigh of relief that he didn't ask him about the 20 dollars or why they left so abruptly.

"Oh, nothing, never mind then. Hey, thanks a ton for the tacos, brotha, you really made my day!"

Andy smiled, "No problem, chief."

There was an awkward silence of fear that each detected the other's secrecy. That silence was broken when

Andy blurted out, "I didn't take that 20 dollars you know," seeking for praise.

"So?" replied Peter.

"Well, I wanted to tell you because I didn't want you thinking I'm some thief, even though I didn't even take it. I mean at first I wanted you to think I was cool, but now, I just don't want you to think that I'm always stealing things, like with that watch."

"Dude, it's whatever, man. I'm not thinking that, so don't worry. Yeah, what was up with that watch anyways?

"Well, like I told you I found it on the sidewalk next to a trash can, it was big, shiny, and looked cool, so I took it."

"Naturally," Peter interjected sarcastically.

"Shut up!" Andy countered, "well, anyways, after I showed it to you then got scared off, some thugs showed up—,"

"The same ones that beat us…or, *me* up?" he interrupted again, asking curiously,

"No. Different ones. So they confronted me and said, 'you took something of ours,' and I just told them they didn't know what they were talking about. So one grabbed me and threw me down on the ground and punched me in the face, hence the black eye that day, but one said 'come on, Ray, he's just a kid!' I yelled 'no I'm not!' and he hit me again in the mouth. Then they all just started searching my pockets. They ripped it out of my pocket, then just ran off and left me there."

"Whoa! Dude, I'm sorry. That's crazy, though!"

"I know, right?" said Andy, then he hesitated for a second, "and then when we were at the car, the reason I wanted to leave so quickly is because I found the watch, or one that looked just like it on the floor, and the face was coming off. So, I picked it up and saw what looked like drugs inside." he ended with a concerned look on his face.

"No way! You didn't take them, did you?"

"No! Of course not! I'm not a junkie!"

"Ok, just checking," Peter quipped.

"But, that's why I wanted to get out of there so fast, because I knew those guys would find me again no problem, and next time they might not be so forgiving. So, since I don't have dying on my list of things to do, I left it there, tossed down the 20 dollars and we bounced; I didn't want to have anything to do with anything there. End of story,"

"That's nuts, my friend. Well, I'm glad you're alright." Peter waited a second, "And I guess since we're 'confessing,' I wanted to tell you about that dog I asked you about. That's who I was talking to when we ran into each other earlier."

"Aha, and does he talk back?" Andy joked.

"No. No, Andy he does not. But anyways I keep running into him and he acts kind of weird, and I don't know what to think about it exactly, but I just kind of follow him around; we just walk around the Town,"

"Hmm, whose dog is it?"

"That, I don't know; he just keeps showing up, and he has a tag on his collar, it just says 'Ketten,' which I'm guessing is his name. I definitely couldn't keep it or anything though, I'd get in trouble."

"That's interesting," replied Andy, seeming to ponder.

"What do you think I should do?" asked Peter hoping to receive some good advice, hoping to find an answer.

"I don't know, man, that's a tough one," he answered, afraid of what Peter would say to his lack of any sort of guidance or answers.

"Alright, I guess I'll just have to see what happens."

Even two years later, Peter is still unsure about Ketten. He doesn't seem to necessarily see any harm coming from having him around. He began to think back again and see if there were any instances in which Ketten *did* in fact cause any harm. He recalled a time earlier in their affiliation, when he had decided since Ketten was always following him around that it would be nice to feed him. So, he started giving him scraps leftover from his meals, and one day Ketten actually bit his hand when he went to give him a piece of meat. Peter remembers it drew blood and hurt really bad. He was too hesitant to discipline him in any way for fear of how he would respond to *that*. Therefore he remained confused and bleeding. He actually yelled at Ketten to try to send him away, but he didn't leave. Instead he just sat there giving Peter a look as if *he* were in charge.

Peter recalled another time when Ketten didn't necessarily cause him harm but he would have allowed it. About a year ago, Peter was wandering the streets again with Ketten by his side, and that particular day things hadn't been received too well on Peter's end. His wandering was interrupted by the confrontation of a frantic man with a hooded jacket, hood on, asking if he had any money. Peter's anger and frustration with the day's events masked his fright, and he responded in an insolent manner saying "does it look like I have any money?" this reaction only pissed the hooded man off more. He revealed a gun tucked in his pants by lifting up his shirt to intimidate and threaten the young Peter, and it worked. Peter, flustered, quickly replied that he had no money at all. The man pushed him down on the ground and called him a "stupid kid," and stormed off. All the while, Ketten stood there backed off a little ways but clearly close enough to witness the whole thing go down. Peter was in awe that this dog, which was apparently his new companion, didn't growl or bark at the man, or try to attack him so as to protect Peter. The man could have shot the boy and according to Peter's observations, he would have been offered zero protection from the aloof canine.

Peter was dismayed by these recollections. Although he indeed felt troubled by these acknowledgements, he didn't feel there was anything he could do. He didn't see a way of getting around his visitations from Ketten. He submitted to the fact that it was a hopeless cause, with only two options: keep running around with Ketten and see what happens, or try to get rid of him and see what happens, the latter proving to be impossible thus far, and not yielding any plausible approaches to accomplishing it either. Distraught, Peter justifies letting him stick around. Abruptly, Peter was visited by a memory, another remembrance of Ketten's behavior, it was recent, only a few weeks previous in fact, and this one was probably the thing that bothered his tender, gentle spirit the most. It was a beautiful day, sun shining, cool breeze blowing, clouds dancing across the sky in slow motion; it was perfect for a hike, of which Peter took full advantage. After exploring the cascading stones, Peter descended with a peaceful high, only to have it disrupted by the next visual by which he would be encountered. As he drew closer to the Town, the sky traded its light in exchange for the darkness, which slowly engulfed the Town.

While there was still enough light left, Peter, on the cusp of the mountainside, was able to spot a striking, bright red cardinal, which at first he thought was wounded, but as he looked a little closer, he saw that it was just rummaging for something to eat. He was captivated. His staring was quickly disturbed when Ketten had leapt out of the bushes, seized the bird in the vice-like grip of its jaws, and shredded its feeble feather armor with his teeth, turning this serene scene into a scene of animalistic ferocity and viciousness. Peter, despite his understanding of how nature works, with its violent, yet *natural*, means of providing sustenance for life, was severely perturbed, with a discontented look of shock and utter astonishment on his face that had at once replaced his previously docile demeanor. He was taken aback; not only was he startled by Ketten's abrupt and unforeseen appearance, but he was troubled that his new "friend" had *completely* destroyed and distorted something he loved. The worst part was that the dog had just walked off, leaving the dead bird bloodied, tattered, mangled and with its head partially attached. Peter was shattered by this sight. He wasn't *entirely* sure why he was so traumatized, but he knew he didn't like it or feel good about it in the slightest. He picked up the bird and laid it in some nearby grass and placed a couple of flowers on its body.

Peter, of course, couldn't help but second guess his decision to keep Ketten around, but as his mind filled with fear, he made no resolve and didn't want to face this predicament; it was too big and too difficult. He wondered how Andy might handle this situation; he remembered back when Andy didn't seem to have any valuable advice or suggestions to offer. Then, he began to wonder if Andy, or anyone else for that matter, had to deal with a problem like this; he couldn't have been the *only* one, he felt. This justifiable thought had downgraded until, he was convinced that he was, in fact the only one who had this kind of issue, therefore, no one had a solution or answers, he concluded. Before being driven mad, Peter decided on a whim to buy a soft-serve ice cream cone because he felt he deserved it. The joy of the ice cream was enough to sustain him for the remainder of his walk home. Once he arrived, he was finally able to carry out his plans. He medicated his troubles with the vibes of steel strings resonating in a wooden body. Peter was improving quite rapidly on the guitar—the guitar he had gotten from Andy's older (more generous) brother, James—which he had always wanted. The mess that had been made and the pile of worries and apprehensions that had been built up, was trampled down by the battering of the vibrations of the beautiful sounds. He found solace this night.

~ CHAPTER 3 ~

THE MOUNTAINS

Peter was now 18. On this day, he was determined to break down his barrier of trepidation and get out of his comfort zone by asking a girl out, or at least for her number, or at the very least for her name, or if all else fails, just saying "hello" would suffice. You see, Peter wasn't the best at communicating in general (which certainly never stopped him from talking), but when it came to girls, he was lucky if even two words in a given sentence correlated at all. He was exerting all his energy to build up his reserve of courage, when *she* appeared; he was graced by her sight and presence. A shot of adrenaline flooded his brain, the shockwaves from his heartbeats reverberated all the way to his fingertips, and he felt weak in the knees. The fear crippled him and he thought about backing out, but he had resolved to do it, so he broke free of the fetter of fear and made his way over to her. He already premeditated the introductory question he would ask.

"Excuse me," he said with both an amazement that he actually did it, and realization that there's no going back now, she promptly turned to face him, "Have we met before? You look really familiar," he asked.

"Um, I don't think we've met, I don't know who you are." She replied awkwardly.

"Oh, I know that actually, I just needed an excuse to talk to you, my name's Peter, what's yours?" he said confidently with a smirk.

The young blonde beauty blushed and replied, "I'm Sarah," with an enormous grin that she could not suppress.

"No way! That's my favorite name! Do you like sushi, Sarah?"

"Uh, yeah. Yes, I do,"

"Rad. Okay, 7pm, Wednesday at TokYoshi Sushi Restaurant, can you make that?" he offered.

"Hold on," she thought for a moment, "yeah, I can make that!" she agreed.

"Sweet!" exclaimed Peter before exchanging phone numbers, bidding farewell and walking away with the biggest smile his cheek muscles could possibly allow…At least this was how it panned out in Peter's head.

In actuality, Peter, still, upon being stricken with immobility and weakness of the joints, *did* in fact break free and attempt to pursue this fine young lady, only as he approached and the words "Excuse me" clumsily stumbled out of his mouth.

Right at the same moment, she yelled "Hey!" with a look of pleasant surprise on her face.

It was in Peter's direction, so he assumed it was to him. Caught off guard, and grinning in a stupor he replied "Uh, hi."

Only to have her dart past him saying, "Bailey! How are you?" to an apparent friend as they hugged.

Peter, submerged in awkwardness and embarrassment, walked away swiftly to escape any further such feelings. After most of the awkwardness and embarrassment trickled out from walking around, he got a chuckle out of the whole situation, a chuckle at the ridiculousness and the seemingly frequent occurrence and repetition of these kinds of happenings.

Then, Peter was relieved from the aftermath of this nonsensical conundrum by the greeting, "What's up, chump?" from his dear friend, Andy. Peter just laughed for a minute until Andy forced him to tell him the meaning of his laughter. As he recounted the events, they found the humor in it all and laughed together about it. This was good for Peter, because had it not been for Andy's impeccable timing and happy-go-lucky spirit, Peter would have continued dwelling on it, permitting it to eat at him, catalyzing the cyclical course of depressiveness, loneliness and beating himself up over false and illusory failures. Peter, ironically, *in* his isolation had developed these malicious behaviors, the toxic roots of which were imbedded deep from many years of unfortunate practice. Peter was grateful for Andy. Andy was unaware of how much he was helping his friend.

Andy was glad to see Peter, "I was actually looking for you though, dude! My brother invited me on a backpacking trip and he told me to ask you if you can, or if you want, to come. So, whaddya say?" he said.

"Aight, when, where and for how long?" Peter inquired.

"Next Wednesday, Canary Peak, 4 days," he chuckled, "So yeah, we'll leave in a week and a half, from Wednesday until Saturday night, there's a trail up North Canyon that leads to this really cool peak and there are some lakes nearby as well, so bring something to swim in, or just nothing if you prefer to swim naked. It's 12 miles round trip, and the trail is pretty decent, not too grueling.

There are some steep switchbacks at one point but they are short, so nothing to worry about, and then we can also climb Canary Peak if you want. Should be pretty fun." Andy described.

"Dude. I'm down. That sounds stellar," Peter said eagerly.

"Great! So it will just be James, you and me. Actually, he did say he was going to try and invite a friend, so we'll see,"

"Sweet, man, I'm stoked!"

"OK chief, if I don't see you before the trip, then take it easy, and I'll be lookin' forward to it! Tschüss!"

Peter giggled, "Alright, me too! Thanks for inviting me, man! See ya," he said, and they parted ways.

Peter already started thinking about how he would prepare and what he would pack for the trip as he walked with an aim to find another opportunity for redemption with a girl, now that he was more hyped up. He was a very shy boy. With each girl that passed him on his path toward home, an excuse why it wasn't an ideal situation to address her and try to introduce himself followed. He tried so hard; the only problem was that these efforts resided merely within his mind, and didn't make it out to see the sunshine much. Paradoxically, his isolation was fed by loneliness.

He also subconsciously trained his brain to resort to pride, anger and—the worst of all—fear, to rationalize, justify, provide comfort for, and remedy his distresses. Little did he know, that it was a *false* comfort and he was only digging himself deeper into this paradoxical pit of these negative feelings and emotions using a shovel made of the *same* negative feelings and emotions. Peter, naïve to these realizations and insights, continued onward, giving up on his hunt for affection with only a slight dampening of his spirits.

The next day while Peter was playing his guitar, he wondered if he should take it on his backpacking trip. He also tried to commit to memory that he should remind himself to bring his iPod with him. Not having any new song or riff ideas come to him, Peter was becoming impatient and bored with playing the same few songs over and over. He decided to go out for a walk hoping that that would perhaps spur on some inspiration. While making a mental list of things he needed to remember for his trip, he ran into Ketten, and the feelings with which he was confronted reflected an apparent sense of expectation to see him, therefore resulting in a nonchalant and almost accepting demeanor. They walked together quietly for some time, until Peter blurted, "I just want a woman to

hold. You know what I'm talkin' 'bout Ketten. I'm talkin'
'bout *real* love." He knew Ketten didn't understand him or
even comprehend his useless attempts to connect with
Ketten, but it helped his thoughts come together when he
verbally expelled them from his mind in somewhat of an
order, and it also helped him feel like he had at least some
form of companionship, even if it was with a *dog*.

Peter, because of the boredom, simply yielded to
being a shadow of Ketten today without problem, for he
had nothing else to do. There was not much (anymore) of a
wonderment or curiosity as much as there was a
numbness, and slave-like obedience to the trails of this
dog. Curiosity originally reeled him in and now fear kept
him bound to Ketten. In the past three years, Ketten had
grown closer and become more and more attached to the
boy, and the frequency and length of their associations
increased. There was also a new development behind the
scenes on Peter's end, the existence of which he was either
ignorant or denied: there was a vague detection of feelings
of humiliation and exhaustion. They didn't particularly do
anything blatantly *wrong*, or at least of this Peter had
perhaps convinced himself or was conditioned to believe,
nor did they do anything arduous, but he began to feel
embarrassed or ashamed of having him around when

people would look upon this otherwise common pair of boy and dog. *He* perceived that the looks he was receiving from these people were rather unpleasant; he thought maybe people just either weren't used to seeing dogs, Ketten stunk, or that he, with the dog, were wandering in places where they were not welcome or not allowed. Alongside the strange ashamedness, he was also quite exhausted and fatigued after their journeys. In any case, this puzzled Peter, but not enough to make him think twice; he just shrugged it off.

Peter spent a considerable amount of time with Ketten each day for the next three days until he had lost track of the days. He still had a few things to buy in preparation for his trip. Though, in his mind, he was convinced that he was more efficient when he procrastinated his tasks until the last minute. The few days of procrastinating wasn't too extreme, since he still had less than a week, but boredom got the best of him and it was as if he was purposely *trying* to procrastinate by seeking out Ketten willingly. Ketten had become a burden, although Peter to this would not admit. Each day, the same basic events would be repeated: he left the house, either with food or buying food in Town, meeting Ketten on the streets and feeding himself and the dog, then they would wander for hours, *always* finding new strange areas of Town, the resulting feelings still proving constant. Peter wondered if Ketten would, or should, come along with him on his trip into the mountains. Not having an answer, he left that up in the air to happen as it may.

On the third day, after a few hours of wandering with Ketten, he looked around to see where he'd ended up this time, and the surroundings actually looked familiar. He was a bit alarmed by this since, to his knowledge, Ketten had never followed him home. With a concerned and perplexed look on his face, he told Ketten, "I'll be off now," and started to navigate the familiar environs towards home, looking around nervously for signs of Ketten following him.

The rest of the week proceeded similarly, until the last day before his trip, he decided he needed to finally end the procrastination and proactively plan, prepare and pack for the departure the next day. In the strain of trying to get things together to begin packing, a flustered Peter decided to take a quick walk to clear his mind in hopes that his organizational skills could be honed in and utilized effectively, and of course, on his walk he ran into Ketten. He tried to fight it, "No! Ketten what are you doing here? I'm just taking a quick walk; I can't spend time with you today. I've gotta pack!" he said. When Ketten started walking one direction, intending that Peter would follow, Peter watched for a few seconds before turning the opposite direction and attempting to sneak off without him noticing. He thought he had outsmarted Ketten and got away. Once he had become lax from being alone again, he sensed a presence prowling nearby; turning to look behind him, he found the dog. Peter, aggravated, scowled at him, and tried to shun him. Ketten growled. He promptly decided he'd had enough fresh air and started running home, both to start packing and to lose Ketten. Ketten responded by chasing him, growling and barking. Peter feared this behavior, for he couldn't determine if it was playful or aggressive. Peter ceased running and slowed to a casual walk so that Ketten would discontinue these actions; and he did. Peter submitted, "Okay, fine. 5 minutes, that's *it*!" he said sharply.

Peter proceeded to waste the majority of the day from that point on with Ketten, becoming lost in the wandering. Once the numbness and false hope in the endless futile search for *something* wore off, he jolted away from Ketten and began swiftly towards home. He beat himself up for having made a huge misstep in indulging in this escape and wasting so much time. He rushed to the store on the way to pick up the few things he needed, grateful that at least the store was still open for a little bit longer. He arrived home carrying this heavy psychological load only to ironically pack up another heavy physical load. This task proved difficult, dealing with *two* burdens, for he was quite distracted; he had distracted himself right out of completing (or even beginning) this task until it was late at night, and he was left only with a pile he created next to his backpack of all the essential items. At this point, Peter, exasperated, gave up and went to bed, firm on finishing quickly in the morning before their departure into the mountains. He was spent and lied down. His head sunk into his pillow, feeling more weighed down than usual.

The next morning, Peter, having slept in, awoke late and feeling rushed. When he noticed the time, he sprung out of bed and at once began the small project of packing as if he was already in the middle of doing it. He heard the honk of a car horn outside; James and Andy were there waiting. This agitated him more, and he shakily tried to speed it up. Luckily, he already had most everything laid out on the floor; it was a matter of double and triple checking and packing it efficiently in the pack. He heard a few more honks outside, to which he replied, "I know, I know! I'm coming!" He threw together all his food along with some breakfast to eat on the way, and he was finished and ready to go. He ran through a mental checklist at the door really quick before leaving. Certain he had everything, he ran out to the car, and was greeted by Andy's sarcasm, "Pardon us for so rudely interrupting your ever so important agenda!"

"Yeah, couldn't you have come *after* my soap operas?" replied Peter wittily. Peter was happy to see them, although he was still mad at himself for allowing this to happen; he didn't like being rushed, and it was his own fault, but he hid these feelings.

"Peter, this chump is my buddy, Buckley, but we call him Buck for short," said James, introducing the friend, who he ended up bringing.

"What's up, little dude?" said Buck.

"Hey man, nice to meet ya," Peter said, breathing heavily still.

All four of them took off in fairly good spirits, or at least ready for the mountain to impart with *them* the good spirits.

The three-hour trip treated them well with plenty of "rocking out to radical tunes," jokes and laughter, sarcastic and witty teasing, and delicious snacks. Upon arrival, they all spilled out of the car and drank in the view of the beautiful mountain range before them; it sobered them right up. In each of their faces you could see the immense impact of the mountains: Buck had wonder spelled out on his face, James had a look of fervor, Andy, a gigantic smile—unable to conceal his excitement—and Peter held a look of inquisitiveness upon his face, intrigued as to what awaited him in the heart of this boulder fortress. They idled no longer and advanced on the 6-mile trail to their destination: Canary Peak.

Suddenly, a mile or so into the trip, it hit Peter that he had forgotten his iPod. Peter was bummed about it, and he expressed his disappointment in his memory, which failed him, "I cannot believe that I forgot it! It would have made the atmosphere of the mountains so much more peaceful! *But,* despite the fact that I forgot my iPod, I am pretty pleased with myself. Given the fact that I packed the entirety of my bag in about .2 seconds, I'm *pretty* sure that I remembered everything." he said joyfully.

"I'm impressed," said Andy.

"Thanks, that means a lot," replied Peter with a grin.

As they moved along, step-by-step, Peter let songs play in his mind to substitute the lack of tangible music, and was quite content with that. The sounds of the music mixed with the sounds of nature (of which there weren't many), and Peter gradually began to grow comfortable and accustomed to listening with open ears, there is much serenity that can be found with letting go and detaching—a fact, with which Peter was becoming acquainted.

After much physical strain, many breaks, loads of water, a few occasional outbursts of singing, and plenty of both deep and light conversations, they finally arrived to their destination. Marveling at the supreme beauty of Canary Peak and its surrounds, Peter, Andy, Buck and James hunted for a nice space to make camp, with the tranquil splendor seeming to lighten their load a bit for the final minutes of their excursion. They found a lovely flattened area, with soft ground, and a circle of rocks for a fire pit, plenty far away from people, where they set up their tents and hammocks and got ready for slumber—since they were bushed—to rest up for the next day's activities. Peter fell asleep happy that night.

The next day consisted of an abundance of relaxed but curious exploration of the expanse, along with some fishing and swimming in the lakes nearby. In this they were able to recuperate enough for the final full day, in which they had in plan to climb Canary Peak. They scoped out the face of the mountain to find a feasible pathway to the top. That night they built a fire, roasted some s'mores and candy, and made up horror stories to tell, which actually just ended in laughter because of how ridiculous they became. Typically, Buck and James mostly kept to each other's company, and Peter and Andy to their own, but they still had fun all together despite the age differences. As they went to sleep the darkness of dusk guided them to their subconscious dreaming.

The next morning, the light of dawn led them out of their dreams and into wakeful consciousness. They arose, and prepared for the climb. With swollen, foggy, tired eyes, they made breakfast and organized a small daypack with enough water and snacks, to sustain them up the 2,000-foot climb. On their way to the base of the mountain, there was only silence, excluding a few singing birds, until one of them started to hum the tune of a Led Zeppelin song. The humming gradually grew louder until another joined in, and louder until finally all joined in the humming, which escalated till the whole song was performed to the end, complete with vocals, and guitar and drum sound effects. Once they finished, no one said anything; they simply kept on the trail, mutually smiling at how cool they thought they were. They reached the base soon after and began the ascent.

All the boys were fairly experienced climbers, so this mountain wasn't too strenuous for them. On the way up, there were a few instances where fear crept in because of the dangerous conditions, but overall the thrill of climbing, testing their abilities and the views trumped the fear. Besides, they were confident in their skills. Peter liked the rocks (rather than earthy ground) when climbing mountains, because they are solid and stable, you don't have to worry about sliding on loose soil and gravel, thus causing a cycle of progression and retrogression; you are simply always progressing. There was plenty of entertainment provided (primarily from the older boys) on the way up the mountain. Peter smiled, embracing the goodness of this trip thus far and predominantly this climb, and thinking that this will surely stick with him for years to come: the laughter, company, sights, smells, and feels. The thought came to his mind that perhaps it was better that he didn't bring his iPod, as it might have been a distraction from these moments.

As they neared the top, Peter had caught glances of the view in his peripherals, but he didn't look; it was as if he was saving the full view for the end when he could see it at its best. They had left quite early in the day and they had the rest of the day free, since this was the only thing in plan for that day, so they took their time, relishing the experience. Once they reached the summit, they were not only at the apex of the mountain, but also at the apex of their emotions; the view and the feelings were overwhelming, and for some reason, it struck them especially strong this time, so much so that it deprived them of speech. They stood motionless for a few minutes, vigorously and observantly scouring the panorama before their eyes, appreciating even the smallest details. Once they felt they had studied the scenery enough, they walked around a bit, hopping from rock to rock, taking looks over the edge, down each side of the mountain.

"I wish I would have brought my camera!" said Peter regretfully, to which James replied, "I'm actually glad *I* didn't, I think sometimes it can be a distraction, and most of the time pictures never do it justice; plus you can usually always find the same images on the internet." Which gave Peter something to think about.

Buck and James paired off and became slightly separated from Peter and Andy, each of whom were having their own conversations. Peter and Andy found a nice spot to sit and partake of their sustenance. A few moments of ingesting the majesty of the magnificence before them had passed before suddenly, something large obstructed their view, a stunning golden eagle soared above them, nearing where the boys were perched, it came and joined them finding a rock of its own, on which to perch. All four boys witnessed and stared intensely at the creature. The boys felt like the glorious bird of prey was sharing some wisdom with them, and when it sensed they were filled, it spread its wings and took to the skies, leaving the boys in awe. They observed until the dark color of the feathers of the bird meshed with the backdrop of the surrounding mountains and was camouflaged. "Did you guys see that?" yelled James to the other boys. They nodded enthusiastically.

"Man, I wish I could fly, just up and fly away out of here at anytime," voiced Peter. Beneath this simple childish dream, lies a heap of unseen root issues that feed and drive this desire to break away.

"I know a guy that does human wing implants, I could hook you up." Andy quipped, avoiding any sort of sensitive exchange.

The sarcasm didn't register with Peter, "I hate my life," he said with a sudden profound realization.

Andy was too surprised to say anything in reply, so he just listened as Peter began to purge and unload.

"I try, Andy. I try. Nothing seems to go my way. I don't know what good I'm doing here. I'm just stuck *living*. I don't know what to *do*. I just don't know…*anything*! I'm just wandering. I'm lost. It feels like the bad in my life largely outweighs the good, and it should be the other way around. I feel…*tainted*. I don't even think I'm grateful to have been born," Peter concluded with a shaky voice, holding back the tears welling up in his eyes to uphold his image of a "man."

"Wow, dude. So, I guess this is one of those 'heart-to-hearts,' huh?" Andy said. He wasn't typically the "counseling" type, but he tried to offer some insight, and provide comfort for his friend, for whom he cared. "I once saw this graffiti on a public restroom that said 'we're all lost.' We all have our stuff, man. We all need help, but just because you're lost doesn't mean you're *lost*, you know what I'm sayin'? And *I'm* glad you're around, because I know I'm not the best person, but I think you keep me in check a little bit; I could be a lot worse, ya know," he consoled, to the best of his ability, which apparently had quite a significant impact on the distraught Peter, who, at that moment, fought the thought, which confronted him in his mind that was telling him "why do *other* people care about me when I don't even care about myself?" Then, he expressed his appreciation for Andy's kind words, holding back more tears, "Well, thanks, Andy I needed that;" he took a deep breath, "I suppose you're right too."

"I know. I always am," replied a cocky Andy, wearing his classic smirk upon his face.

"Man, dude it feels good up here! Thanks again for inviting me, I needed this," Peter stated gratefully.

"Wouldn't have been the same without ya, we needed *someone* to make fun of," he joshed.

"Let's go explore!" barked Peter excitedly, and they went to climb around atop the field of boulders sprinkled along the ridge of this mountaintop. As they navigated their way around the rocks, they neared a particularly dangerous part; Peter indicated, "This is pretty sketchy," acknowledging the risk, while still accepting the challenge, to which Andy retorted, "All the better!" without hesitation. Peter laughed.

"You see, my philosophy is: in order to know you're living, you have to meet death; sit down with him face-to-face and have a conversation with him, tempt and taunt him, welcome him, but don't let him stay," lectured Andy.

Peter gave an intrigued look and joked, "Oh, so you've met him? Is he nice? So you guys just get together and have a cup of hot cocoa and shoot the bull?"

"Nah, he likes chocolate milk or orange juice better," Andy played along.

They snickered.

Peter looked back, and seeing Buck and James still sitting and conversing, asked Andy, "What do you think they're still talking about?"

"I don't know, man. They are probably discussing the phenomenon of the gravitational collapse of the core of a massive degenerate star…either that, or they're talking about the girls they've made out with." Andy answered aloofly.

"Wow, Andy, I'm impressed! I had no idea you were capable of such scientific profundity!"

"I know. I'm the coolest person on this planet."

"Well then, if you're so intelligent, might you be able to answer me why the devil the word "laugh" is spelled the way it is?"

"Such a nonsensical question, why do you bother troubling yourself with such outlandish foolishness?"

"Hey, I'm just trying to find answers to the things that trouble me deeply—the questions of my soul. Things like that and why cows drink milk."

"Cows drink milk?" replied a repulsed Andy, "Isn't that like, cannibalism?"

"My thoughts exactly," said Peter.

They both laughed.

"You goons ready to go?" James yelled to the younger boys.

"Yeah, fool, after we're done rollin' some boulders down this mountainside!" answered Andy.

"Well, I'm not so sure that's such a good idea, ya know and, okay!" James agreed, without much persuasion, and like the rebellious, rowdy, and reckless youngsters they were, they had a grand time, laughing and curiously examining what happens when falling stones clash against stationary stones; they both cheered and were in awe at the sight. Not a word was uttered from any soul of the small clan of comrades on the way down. A few smiles were peppered throughout the return journey. They all left with a feeling that they had given and taken, forsaken and received, renounced and accepted, let go and moved on, and finally, that no longer were they *carrying* burdensome mountains, they were just climbing them.

They laid to rest for the night in peace, and the light of the sky as they awoke harmonized with the light in their souls, brightening the day. Before packing up, they all lied awake soaking in the nirvana, afraid that if they leave it, it might diminish. Once they were ready to face their departure out of the mountains, they packed up and, taking one final look, bid farewell to the sweet mountains, with which they've bonded; the refuge, which they've enjoyed. The mountains seemed to smile back, grateful for *their* presence. The only noteworthy things that occurred on the trip back to the car were that Peter's shoelace from one boot caught on the shoelace hook of his other boot, causing him to trip and fall flat on his face with the weight of his exhausted body and his pack dragging him down quickly; gravity was punishing. Peter lied there for a moment, not wanting to move, almost as if he'd been waiting for something exactly like this to happen to justify him giving up; for, to give up he indeed wanted due to the fatigue and soreness from the previous days' activities and the opposition he'd faced after the high he just experienced. Andy, Buck and James helped him up and tended to him, "You alright, man?" asked Andy. Peter sat there, staring down, shed a tear, took a deep breath, stood up and they were on their way as if nothing happened, because that's who Peter is.

Also, that Buck had apparently been profoundly impacted by the visit to the mountains, as he shared a thought, "Ya know, the mountains are wise. They've witnessed a lot, they've been around for ages. They've also endured a lot. They've stood firm through countless storms and beatings from different variants of weather and just *nature*. They, like us, are also broken down, torn apart and dealt an array of challenges, but yet they still stand, and not once do they complain," to which all of the boys nodded in agreement and surprise at this wise insight.

Once they arrived to the car, they were relieved, and, although still tired, after a quick nap during the travel home, they were back to their rowdy selves: singing, yelling, teasing and laughing. When they were back in civilization, Peter noticed two girls in the car next to them at the stoplight with their windows rolled down. He rolled down his window and yelled, "Hey! You're cute!" They giggled and one of them blew him a kiss. He didn't say anything in return. He just blushed and grinned, while his friends mocked him. Even though he knew he'd probably never see these girls again, he still felt accomplished.

~ CHAPTER 4 ~

FRIENDSHIP & ENMITY

Peter was 20. He was what you'd call an extroverted introvert, in the right situation and setting, he was loud, outgoing, cracked jokes, and quite frankly most people likely saw it as obnoxious, which is comical, seeing as Peter typically thought other people, whom he observed in public, which did the same things, were extremely obnoxious. Most of the time, however, he was quiet, shy, kept to himself and wouldn't say much unless prompted by another person; in other words, he reciprocated well. In reality, that's how Peter really was: an animated, witty, cheerful and hyperactive guy, young at heart; only, his burden of years of conditioned fear, self-consciousness and resentment towards people, hindered him from letting that shine through. Perhaps this was related to the reason Peter kept his supply of close friends to a minimum, in other words, Andy was his only friend. He had a few friends that he'd picked up along the way, with whom he didn't spend much time though. That is also the reason he talks a lot; he's constantly thinking, and all of these thoughts get stored, but never (or rarely) shared. He likes staying in his comfort zone, and the ideal circumstances for that include having friends whom he can trust and who understand him, which in *his* mind, are hard to come by; an idea fed to him by fear. On top of all that, Peter was just a simple person; simply put.

Peter and Andy had recently been spending a lot more time together. They were devising new shenanigans to quench their overabundance of manic rowdiness. This meant that they had tendencies of being an annoyance to others, terrorizing people (not causing any harm of course) in public. Many thought they were jerks for the things they did, but in their minds, they figured that if they weren't harming anyone, then what was the problem, they took it upon themselves to try and teach people to laugh; even at the irritations in life, because "they *needed* it," and because they felt they should learn that there's no point in getting angry, even at some boorish ignoramus children's mischiefs, since *getting* angry only *makes* you angry.

They started off simple by attaching a $5 bill to a fishing line and setting it in the middle of a hallway, with ample foot-traffic, of an office building, which they snuck into. Then, as soon as some gullible office worker would spot it, they would yank the line, luring him or her to chase the money, thus looking like a fool, leaving Peter and Andy (hidden around the corner) laughing at the man's expense, as they always did. After only a few minutes of waiting, they attracted the attention of one dopey businessman; they laughed as they yanked the money at his each attempt to snatch it up. Then something happened, the man, in his undeterred tenacity to obtain the five dollars, ran head-first straight into the stomach of a tall, rather attractive female office assistant, who was carrying a stack of papers and files in one hand, and a cup of coffee in the other. She, in utter shock, and from the crash, dropped her stack of files, but luckily was able to save her coffee. Peter and Andy exploded in the quietest boisterous laughter possible, since the results of this prank had vastly exceeded their expectations. The man was flush with embarrassment, as he nervously helped clean up the papers and received a scolding from the woman. Peter and Andy were severely pleased with the outcome, toppling out of the office building in a fit of uncontainable laugher.

Amidst all of these pranks with Andy, Peter's relationship with Ketten was also having some developments. He figured since he was spending so much time with him physically, he might as well spend time with him emotionally and intellectually too. He began devoting all of his efforts to let all of the bottled up burdens of life spill out, strictly to Ketten. He isolated himself from other sources of relinquishment, and fixated solely on Ketten, using him as an escape, emancipating himself of these stresses for Ketten to take hold of them. He found comfort in this. He began to think that he *liked* spending time with Ketten, especially since they had been venturing to new destinations. Although, doing this led to greater exhaustion, numbness, and disarray; their bond grew stronger, and Ketten himself was growing stronger being fed not only by food, but also by the pangs of Peter's struggles. Almost daily these visits took place. They came about whether by loneliness, boredom, depression, fear or anger.

Luckily, at least as of late, Andy had been catching Peter when he was weighed down by these feelings; they had suddenly become obsessed with these pranks. The next one they wanted to try had to do with water balloons. They filled up a whole basket and went to a crowded area in the Town center, and off to the side, they chucked balloons, one after another, as hard and high as they could into the mass of humans. When they heard the screams and the yelling of wonderment as to from where, by who, what or how this atrocity happened, they roared with laughter.

In between throws, Andy conversed with Peter. "So, I've been seeing this girl."

"Oh yeah? Dude that's amazing, I didn't even know you *liked* girls!" teased Peter.

Andy laughed, "Thanks...but yeah, bro, she's pretty dang great though. Super cute, outdoorsy, smells good, and she's just a *good* person," he said as they each threw another balloon.

"She sounds like a gem. Seriously!" Peter validated.

"Yeah," Andy paused, "but I'm afraid,"

"Of what?"

"Well, I fear that *because* she's so good, that I won't match up to what she wants or needs. I mean, what's gonna happen when she finds out about the things I've done, or am doing?" Andy expressed worriedly.

Peter didn't ask about what he was "doing," but he kind of assumed what it may be, but didn't need to know, "Maybe that's what you need, homie?"

"I don't know, man, maybe I do need that, but I think *I'm* fine, I'm just more worried about her, I don't want to, like, *corrupt* her or something." He threw a balloon.

"Nah, dude. You're a good guy, Andrew Locke," said Peter as they smiled at each other just about as comfortably as two men showing affection to each other possibly could. To end the awkwardness, they each grabbed what was left of the water balloons and unloaded on the innocent citizens, laughing all the while. Their laughter was interrupted by the blaring howl of one of the victims, "HEY!" realizing they'd been spotted and were about to become victims themselves, they booked it, though still highly entertained by the man's reaction and the chase. They got away safely in the end.

On the flip side of this amusement lied some disconcerting happenings on the Ketten front. Peter was continually enjoying his company and all the while disclosing the thoughts, feelings and distresses, which he kept private, save during his encounters with the dog. One night, they were walking; they walked and walked. Peter was lost in the mechanical daze, deeply immersed in the spell, which Ketten—or whatever it was—had over him. Thoughts, upon arrival to his mind, were dispensed with no filter, or care of what became of them; anyone listening to his one-ended conversations would have an honest look into the depths of the chasms of the landscape that was his mind.

Then, something snapped in Peter's mind, as had sometimes happened, where he suddenly became frustrated with Ketten and the pointlessness of their wanderings, and he blamed Ketten for his troubles, "You don't even care about me, what are we even doing out here? What do you want from me?" he demanded. Ketten growled and gnashed his teeth, his hair standing up on his back; this time Peter tested this display of anger, "What are you gonna do?" he yelled in return, convinced that the dog wouldn't dare try anything, only to have Ketten lunge at him barking piercingly, "Piss!" Peter screamed, dodging the attack and sprinting away. He found a good-sized stick for defense and turned to face Ketten. The dog was *ravaging*, and Peter's opposing attacks in self-defense seemed only to feed the canine's rage. Peter was quite successful in blocking the dog's bites with the stick, deflecting the lunges and forcing the stick into his mouth, when finally, after pushing him off, in fatigue he cried out, "Okay, STOP!" holding out his hands, yet still grasping the stick, "okay, okay, okay, okay, it's okay!" he tried to negotiate. Ketten ceased his attacks although continued to growl. Peter dropped the stick, "okay, it's alright, everything is o-kay," not knowing what else to say. The dog stared at him, slowly easing into withdrawal, whilst Peter became less and less tense as the moments crawled by. "Jeez, what's your problem?" Peter muttered. Ketten huffed.

The dog was obviously becoming angrier, undoubtedly to indicate to Peter that he had total control over him, which Peter bought, hence the submission of fear. However, it *did* appear that no matter what Peter tried, the dog always had a counter; the more Peter gave in, the more susceptible he was to giving in, and as long as Peter didn't disrupt the cycle, it was a cyclical self-strengthening process. A few days following the display of rage, Ketten seemed to be on edge at every little thing; Peter wondered if this would linger. Ketten snapped at him—scathing his skin with his teeth—even when Peter tried to pet him, and another time when he was feeding him some leftovers. This was becoming a real problem. Peter's physical countenance was affected thereby.

Thankfully for Peter, Andy was there to lift him and his countenance. Andy came quickly and eagerly to snatch Peter up to go satiate their newfound cravings to lightheartedly bully innocent people, in other words to prank and in so doing teach them a "valuable lesson," and

have a great deal of fun in the process (in *their* eyes).
Andy had one last idea (at least for now), which came to
him when he was at the thrift store and saw a costume that
looked like an old mascot suit. They bought the costume
and found another sort of getup for Peter to wear to
disguise their identities, their destination: the local golf
course. They arrived and found a bush, behind which to
hide, scoping out their targets, then, when the timing was
right—right when the oblivious golfer putted—they
sprung out of the bushes, dressed in their ridiculous getup,
ran and kicked the golf ball before it plunged into the hole.
Howling with laughter, they escaped the enraged golfer's
chase and swinging golf club. They spent quite a long time
on the golf course doing these kinds of tomfooleries along
with chasing golf carts, sneaking up behind concentrated
golfers and hugging them or slapping them on the butt ,
and dancing to distract and infuriate the golfers. They
stayed, that is, until the administration was informed and
started hunting them down in the hottest pursuit a golf cart
could give. They split up and of course were never caught
due their masterful skills in dodging and evading. Peter
and Andy were the best of friends and this time well spent
only strengthened their bond.

Unfortunately, the high Peter was on didn't last too long; he was just having a rough time throughout the past few weeks, facing some hefty opposition. He did what he had learned, or been conditioned to do; he turned to Ketten. At that time, he had just given up trying. He had fallen hard into the grasp of Ketten. He had spent the entirety of three days straight at one point, only coming home very late at night for a few hours, to sleep, and not well at that. Peter's appearance reflected his inner feelings, which he was battling, or rather, to which he had become a casualty, so to speak. He succumbed under the pressure. He wore his backpack with a few items, a book and food since he was gone all day, and quite possibly would end up sleeping out on the streets. His backpack seemed to contain much more than that; it seemed to be full of all of the burdens, misfortunes, mistakes, questions, doubts, fear, anger and any other adverse influence, which had accrued over the two decades of his life. This was a heavy affliction, by which he was weighed down and impeded; it was a real encumbrance. He was *numb*. Peter's eyes were fastened to the ground like a train bound to the tracks, following mindlessly the path of Ketten, as he led Peter deeper into the darker concourses of the Town. As Peter's pace slowed subconsciously, Ketten would growl, frustrated therewith, to induce a quickening of pace, keeping him close.

The next thing Peter knew, he awoke from unconsciousness, lying facedown on a street, which was tucked away, out of sight from any unlikely late-night passersby. He sat up; he felt cold and very confused. His memory did not serve him well, as all he could remember was wandering late in the darkness, not ever looking up to even be able to recognize where he was; he was completely lost in the confines of the depths of the darkness of the Town. His memory faded into nothingness, supplying no answer as to how he ended up where he was; only a wide gap remained between when he last remembered walking behind Ketten to awaking in the street. He didn't feel any pain, eliminating the possibility of an attack. Still attempting to gather any evidence of the situation, he noticed that Ketten had apparently disappeared. This irritated Peter. He took hold of that fact, and clung to it, lashing out and blaming Ketten for *everything* wrong that had happened in his life. The irritation grew; he was angered. Sputtering out senseless babbling, Peter felt betrayed, hurt and certainly alone. Peter was infuriated. He beat himself up too for being the "idiot" that allowed Ketten to enter his life and stay. Peter was faced with just about every negative emotion in this instance. He sat down on the curb and sulked, with thoughts from each end of the spectrum rushing through his mind, he let his gaze rest on the ground while the thoughts played out in front of him. Once the display of images and thoughts had concluded, Peter decided he'd better stand up and move. Not knowing what time it was, how long had passed since he "passed out," or even since he'd awoke, and still not knowing where he was, he determined he should walk around down some different streets so he could identify where the mountains were in relation to his current location. The mountains were a good compass.

Dumbfounded by this mishap, Peter contemplated the worthwhileness of keeping Ketten company. It hit him that he didn't actually *have* to keep Ketten around; he could choose *not* to spend time with him. Peter, fed up with the ludicrous nature of their relationship—to which he had been so negligent—committed to stop seeing Ketten; he was at least resolute on *his* end, that he would not seek him out, but as for the dog's end of things, he wasn't sure how to handle that. He figured maybe he'd have to develop new habits, or replace his time that he usually spent with Ketten with different projects or activities. This was going to prove to be quite a feat, since Ketten's presence had been a plague for so long, but a plague *welcomed* by Peter however, for purposes of comfort, which was a farce all along, although he did not see it. Peter cycled through his emotions from determination, to fear, to sadness (for he was not sure if he was ready to let go), to anxiety and back to determination. He was going to try it.

~ CHAPTER 5 ~

THE OLD FRIEND

Peter is now 23. He lie on his bed in his room, hands behind his head, staring upward, his stare penetrating the ceiling, probing for something, something to which he could attach: an idea, a concept, a *reason*…an answer. There was a thick silence. Ketten lies next to him on the floor, head up, ears perked, panting, alert. The lyrics of a familiar and favorite song of Peter's cleared the fog of silence and reached in and saved him from drowning in the dejection on his bed. Peter forgot he had his music playing; he wondered how long he'd been "out." He sat up and looked at Ketten, not a smile or a grimace, but an expressionless, *dead* gaze rested on his face. Ketten's response was a reciprocal blank stare. Just as there was silence perceived by Peter despite the music playing, there was darkness despite the light on in his bedroom. Silence. Darkness. Isolation. Ketten his only companion. He stood up and walked over to his mirror, "How did it get to this?" he asked himself in his mind, staring at the reflection of a grayish-colored skin, drooped eyes, with bags under them. He looked again at Ketten in the mirror. Then he glanced at his guitar in the mirror and thought he'd sit and play on it.

"Why do you struggle during a storm to see the blue sky, when the clouds are inevitable? / Just let it all pass by, and you'll gain a stronger eye," he sang. Peter was much more talented when it came to writing the music; tunes would simply come to him, and he would play what sounded good. However, when it came to writing song lyrics, his skill level was subpar, but every once in a while, certain phrases would pop up in his mind, which he would then work into the songs, which he played. He played and sung loudly until the vibes crushed him and he was reduced to tears. Ketten was never enthused by his melodies and would hide himself up in Peter's closet, or go outside or something, whenever he would play.

Later that night, Peter went out on a walk. At this point in his life, it was unavoidable that anywhere he would go, Ketten was constantly by his side, and this problem was at its worst. Peter was humiliated and ashamed of having him around, in public and particularly in places where dogs weren't typically allowed, seeing as he could do nothing to dismiss the dog, Ketten remained by his side, and if he was confronted by a shop owner, or employee, he eventually just started claiming that it was a service dog to avoid the hassle, since Ketten was not a pleasant animal—even to Peter—especially not with strangers, which usually allowed a prolonged stay. Peter is in the pits; he's in the depths, hovering above rock bottom. Inside he's looking for a ladder, a way out, but yielding no obvious results. The search remains very monotonous and hopeless. He wanders. Deep down he feels the part of him, yelling, struggling to break free, but is being pinned down, powerless against the clutches of the other part of him, which has grown strong and now dwarfs the former part.

This has been a development over the span of about a year and a half. A significant and traumatic event occurred, which completely shattered his previous commitment—from another year and a half earlier, when he was 20—to refrain from walking with Ketten, which his efforts were *religious* to keep. Once he made that commitment, something in him awoke, and he drew strength and incentive therefrom. He did good. He was able to distance himself from Ketten, and change his environment and behavior so as to prevent any encounter with his newly made enemy. He played guitar more often, he went on more hikes, he bought a camera and started to pick up photography, he started learning Japanese, and he even started playing soccer with a city recreational team, since he had always wished he could play. He was feeling good. He spent a lot of time indoors, and if he was outside, it was in the mountains where Ketten never seemed to follow, or amongst a big group, so he practically never saw the dog. There was a few instances where he saw him afar off, but it was after a game and he climbed into a friend's car hurriedly to head home, escaping Ketten's presence.

At the beginning of this transformation of sorts, it was rather difficult for Peter, to remain devoted and diligent, but after a couple weeks, habits were developed and efforts became natural and the outcome made it worthwhile. He felt *lighter* and more clarity. Although, he did, in fact, recognize these contrasting feelings, it was easy to forget how it feels when one is entrenched and *captured* by another entity. He waxed and waned in his persistent efforts to keep himself away from the dog. He wavered in his vision of being free. He gradually allowed the same stresses to penetrate his barriers, which he had formed, and though he did not fall back into his old ways, and resort to his old habits, he was surely on the path, which would lead to such an end, unaware, however. His lone efforts carried him quite a distance; his self-discipline and separation from Ketten lasted in total for about a year and a half. The gradual decline began after the year mark—nearing his 22nd birthday. However, *nothing* could have prepared him for what he was about to then experience.

On this particular day, Peter was on his way back from a soccer game, it was a good game; he was pretty pleased with the improvement of his skills. After the game, he changed his clothes and put on his backpack, and started towards home by foot. He normally would get a ride from a friend, but it didn't work out that day, due to an illness of one of the guys, and all the other cars being full. The other players and chauffeurs apologized profusely, despite the fact that Peter was perfectly fine with walking home. He loved walking. He hadn't given heed to the possible threat of running into Ketten, however. He was rather content walking around outside, since it had been a while, so he decided to take a path that differed a little from his typical route home from where he was. He, as always, allowed his thoughts to run through his head, occasionally chuckling out loud when a humorous memory from the earlier game came to mind.

It was dark, and wet from previous rainfall. Peter rounded the corner of a building; he came up to a side street where something caught his attention. To the right of him, the dim light was blanketed over a figure lying in the street; his attention was caught by the figure's moaning. He stopped, and hesitated helping (because you never know who is involved, people have learned, unfortunately, to stay away, since sometimes it may cause you more trouble than it's worth), he knew he should, but didn't know what to do. Suddenly, he heard the figure call out, "Peter?" Peter was stunned. Hearing his name called out from the figure was like taking a blow from a sledgehammer in the gut, for that meant it could only be one person. This realization that the person must have been Andy, lying in the street, apparently severely wounded, hit Peter like a hurricane of all sorts of overwhelming emotions. He came to after a few seconds of trying to accept the unbelievable reality before his eyes and trying to process it all.

Once it registered, he dropped his backpack and ran over, stumbling, weeping and in shock. Andy lie, head propped up on the curb, with his hand over a bloodied spot on his shirt on his abdomen, "Peter, what's good, homie?" he said with his classic smirk on his face. His voice and body was weak; it looked like he'd been there for some time now. Peter ignored his satirical optimism, how he still mocked pain and death—even as he lie in its very grasp.

"Andy, what happened? How long have you be— who did this? Where are they now?" Peter said frantically, breathing rapidly and scrambling to figure out how he could help.

"Peter, Peter. Always so quick to fix things," Andy said weakly, slowly, shaking his head, "Do you not see me lying here in front of you? I don't care and it doesn't matter."

Peter kept looking at him like he was crazy, "We gotta get you—"

"Peter! Why are you so *afraid*?" interrupted Andy a bit more sternly, "It's like I'm *dying* and you don't even care."

Peter had nothing to say to that. Taken aback and frustrated, he asked, "So, what do you want me to do then?"

Andy looked at him with an approving smile, "*Be here* with your friend,"

"I *am* here," said Peter, slightly confused and annoyed, but submissive.

He nodded, accepting his response, "Be here," he repeated, whispering with his eyes closed.

A few moments passed, Peter let the disbelief and anxiety dissipate, and when it cleared out, he felt calm.

"That's right," said Andy, still with closed eyes.

Peter was puzzled at how Andy seemed to sense that he calmed down. Then, just as quickly as he calmed down, he fell straight back into the fear and anxiety, thoughts rushing through his mind, of how he's going to manage, what this is going to mean for him now, and why is this happening. Tears welled up again, and trickled down his cheek.

Andy chimed in, again somehow appearing to sense Peter's distress, "Peter, why does it seem like *you* are the one in more agony right now?" he scoffed, "This isn't going to change anything," he confirmed.

"How can you say that?" Peter retorted.

"I just know." He paused, "I've always been the smarter of the two of us," he smirked.

Peter shook his head, still crying. He heard the words Andy was saying, but he didn't allow himself to *listen.*

Andy shuffled a little bit, trying to shift his position, groaning with pain, still holding the wound on his stomach. "Listen…just remember: when you think you can't, you *can*." He tilted his head back, and closed his eyes again. His breaths came more infrequently and were quite sparse.

Peter, slightly irritated and frustrated, wondered what his words meant, convincing himself that he had completely lost it and didn't know what he was saying.

Andy started speaking again, very faintly, "Tell James thanks, sorry and I love him. Tell the rest of my family the same, and tell Peter…tell Peter the same thing too."

Peter wept.

"Tell Peter not to worry."

He was slipping away. Peter could tell. Many things flushed through his mind that he could say, or that he wanted to say to his departing friend. There were too many things, unable to settle on any one in particular, he finally replied, still weeping, but with however much of a smile he could muster, "Right back at ya, buddy," but when he looked at Andy's face, it appeared that it was too late. Peter collapsed beside his friend, as the tears finally burst through; he was crushed. Andy had left.

He stayed there and wept for what seemed like hours. Practically inconsolable, Peter was paralyzed by the devastating travesty. A range of emotions plunged into his heart and mind like daggers being thrown at him from all sides. He felt distraught, then angry, then severely morose, then calm, then anger again, then bewilderment, and so on. Eventually, apparently some passerby or nearby resident who heard the cries from the scene alerted the authorities and the people in charge of "caring for" the unfortunate victims to the Town's perpetrators and antagonists came to take Andy away. Peter sobbed more at the sight of his departed friend departing, for good this time. He sat down curled up on the curb and remained for the rest of the night, mourning, even into the morning.

Once Peter had picked himself up and put himself back together, he decided it was probably wise to head home, but he had no desire and didn't want to see or talk to anyone. When he arrived home, he only retrieved his iPod and left. He was looking for something, a way out. He was trying to break away, to run, to fill the void. He knew no other way how. As he headed back into the streets again, now with his music, there was Ketten, sitting, ready to take him away, like an old friend. He had no physical or emotional reaction to their meeting, although he did half-expect to see him. He knew inside that it probably wasn't the best route to take, but it was the "*only*" route to take, and he was sort of subconsciously searching for him anyway. With his hands in his hoodie pocket, hood on, head down, Peter entered the "state of Ketten," so to speak. He was numb. Peter had hit rock bottom. There was much in Peter's life that had bottled up and that he hauled around, leaving him vulnerable and though he might've denied it, teetering on the edge, where even a smaller affliction would have likely sent him toppling over the edge. He had fallen and he had fallen harder than ever before. This was the most difficult trial of his life.

This meeting with Ketten was only the beginning of a descent, the gateway to total loss. For the better part of the next two months, Peter was dragged down by Ketten, so much so that he would disappear for hours, and even days. They wandered. Weaving in and out of stranger and stranger paths, Peter, at times, found himself staring in the darkest abysses, which he had not known existed in the Town. Peter usually returned feeling ill, if he even returned at all. As they walked, Peter would occasionally see things that would *typically* cause him to rupture with boisterous laughter, but at this point, didn't even make him crack a smile. Even things like a thief stealing a lady's purse, but almost immediately after he snatched the bag, he ran into a pole, fell to the ground, and the lady picked up her purse, kicked the thief, and kept walking. Another time he saw a drunken man's pants, *and* underwear, fall to the ground. He saw some nerds sword fighting in a park, doing a live-action-role play. The best was a man eating and severely enjoying an ice cream cone, who then sneezed, smashing his face into the ice cream. All of these hilarious antics would be funny for anyone and would cheer up even a pouting child, but nothing could medicate Peter as he was in a funk that was ostensibly incurable and irredeemable.

Ketten kept Peter close, and (although highly infrequent) whenever Peter would try to go his own way, Ketten's anger would manifest itself. Ketten was ruthless in taking charge and showing dominion over Peter. Peter followed willingly. This was the beginning of Ketten's constant companionship that continued up to the present, in which he is 23 years of age. This dog, which had been following and leading him to some degree since he was 12, had Peter trapped like a fish with no tail or fins caught in a fisher's net.

A few days after the passing of Andy, it was time for the funeral. This was the only social gathering of *any* sort, at which he was present during those two months of exile. Peter showed up, but it was evident that *Peter* wasn't really there. He was grudgingly moping at the loss of his best friend. He still was under the impression that Andy was insane and blabbering nonsensically at the time of his passing; he was clearly not taking this well at all. Fear and anger clouded his judgment. There was quite a scarce number in attendance. Only his family (obviously including James, beside whom stood Buckley), a few family friends and other relatives, which Peter didn't know, except for one of Andy's uncles, that he met once and is a cool guy. Other than that, there was only the funeral director and another peculiar man, dark-haired, bearded, old and dressed in a black suit, which stood not amongst the family, whom Peter also did not know.

Peter was angry, taking personal offense at Andy's death; he couldn't figure out where this anger was directed though: at himself? Was it at Andy? Or was it directed at Andy's killers? They had found out that it was most likely the drug thugs, who had taken Andy's life. It wasn't 100% confirmed, but projected to be the most accurate. Peter had secretly known—or presumed—that Andy was involved, in one way or another, with drugs. However, it seemed that Andy, in an effort to support his family, got involved with drugs to get some extra money. He had only used a few times earlier on, but never became hooked, as he experienced unpleasant reactions. Andy always *was* a risk-taker; he liked to push the limits.

The funeral commenced, and the director welcomed the Locke family, and any other family and friends who came to pay their love and respects to Andrew Desmond Locke. Peter stared at the casket; as he did, he felt an odd sensation as though he *himself* was in actuality lying in the casket. The funeral director read some nice things (including a hopeful story of a similar situation), and set the tone for a peaceful farewell to a beloved young man. Many tears were shed, but most of which were more out of comfort and peace. Peter made eye contact (although not changing the expression on his face, which reflected his inner turmoil) with a couple of Andy's family members who were happy to see him there. As he looked around, Peter noticed the peculiar man, weeping at the loss of this young man. Peter showed a bit of spite towards this unknown, undeserving man, thinking he had no right to be here, that his presence tainted the feeling of the funeral. At the conclusion of the funeral, James came to console Peter, asking how he was holding up and such, putting his arm around his shoulder. Peter only responded with body language and head nods. Once it looked like he was in the clear to leave, Peter didn't hesitate and headed straight towards Ketten, which he saw off in the distance. The only thought left swirling around in his head as he treaded the path towards his captor, was "who was that man?"

~ CHAPTER 6 ~

THE TURNAROUND

Peter stands motionless at the edge of a dark road at night, staring down a corridor of buildings. Ketten begins growling and barking, and Peter disinterestedly begins walking, still aimed at the other end of the road. With the beat of each step, thoughts hummed a rhythm that created the somber soundtrack, to which he'd been listening for a while now. There was no emotion that became attached to the thoughts, for now they were just floating, just there, playing over and over in his head. These thoughts consisted of all the things Peter remembered that Andy said to him before passing. He doesn't quite know what to make of them. He doesn't quite know what to make of anything for that matter. He quickly entered a state of despondency and sat on the ground. Everything seemed to be foggy and moving in slow motion. Ketten growled and barked again, and even reached out and bit Peter's hand, "Ow! What the frick, dog?" Ketten backed up a couple steps and gave a low growl. "I'm sitting right here and not moving, so don't try to make me go anywhere!" said Peter stubbornly, to which Ketten actually listened. Then Peter's thoughts shifted to that peculiar man. He had forgotten about him since after the funeral. He remembered him vividly. He remembered thinking how he looked similar to Abraham Lincoln, minus the hat. So many questions revolved around this man and his purposes.

As Peter was in a stupor of contemplation, and Ketten was wandering up ahead, a ways off from Peter, he was unprepared for the psychotic hoodlum antagonizing unsuspecting innocents, for which Peter was a prime target. This man ran up and jumped Peter from behind, tackling him to the ground, Peter landed funny on his arm, in which he felt a sharp pain instantly when he hit the ground, he screamed while the attacker and he squirmed around on the ground, "Why don't you stop it and get outta here!" Peter said struggling to get free, the attacker struggling to evidently cause harm. They flipped so that they were positioned facing each other, Peter saw the crazed look in his eyes, messy hair, rancid smell, and figured he was probably drugged up pretty substantially. The man held a knife and yelled, "Prepare for your death!" with a bit of a deranged smile. Peter wriggled his other arm free and punched him in the face. The man was fairly scrawny, he yelped and fell off of Peter and just got up and ran off. Peter thought he heard a faint laughter as he disappeared into the night.

Peter lie in confusion for a few moments, and chuckled through his nose, shaking his head at how random and ridiculous that was. He writhed in pain, sat up and held his right arm; he'd never broken a bone, but he was sure that's what this pain as well as the obtuse angle of his arm was telling him. He was more annoyed at the fact that he'd have to go to the hospital and get this taken care of, and deal with a broken arm than he was at the psychopath who *caused* the broken arm. Peter was rather stubborn when it came to medication or visiting the hospital; he was more of a naturalist, just letting everything run its natural course. This, however, he figured needed medical attention. Bitterly, after a while off contemplating whether he should just try to brace it himself and let it heal on its own, he got up and made his way to the hospital. The nurse was extremely patronizing and belittling towards Peter—at least according to his perception—to which Peter retorted with an array of snarky remarks. From an outside perspective, it would have been a comical exchange.

She asked what happened, he relayed that a deranged man was to blame, and she replied that the "Witnesses" brought in a man just only a few minutes ago, that very well could have been the exact same man. She explained that they found him passed out on the street, with a bloody nose, bloodshot eyes and a gash on his forehead—presumably from falling over when he passed out.

"He was very smelly," she said grimacing. She told him they stitched up his forehead, cleaned him up a bit, gave him some medication and let him rest for now.

"Yep, that's gotta be him. So, wait, what are you going to do with him? You're not just going to let him go are you?" asked Peter, hungry for justice.

"Hon, I just said the *Witnesses* brought him in, did you pop an eardrum too?" she remarked sarcastically.

"Yeah, and?"

She was unenthused by his ignorance, and left him hanging.

"Who are these bloody '*Witnesses*'?" he demanded loudly.

"The Witnesses are the Judge's 'helpers,' I suppose you could say. They sort of take the place of the police: they help regulate the actions of the Townspeople—,"

"Well they are certainly doing a wonderful job!" he interjected sarcastically and spitefully, his eyes motioning to his arm.

"Well, the thing is, sweetheart, that is kind of the point of their job. They aren't hovering over us like the police, waiting to pounce, punishing our every mistake, *but, like* the police they *are* there for our benefit, to protect and serve, just in a more 'invisible' way. What they do is *observe*—hence the term 'Witnesses'—and when they determine that the people are 'ready,' they snatch them up and bring them to the Judge for him to determine what happens to them. There are other towns that have a 'police' system, or other similar systems to oversee the people's doings, but our Town is run a little differently," she said—all the while treating his arm.

Questions were popping in Peter's head like popcorn kernels. "So, wait. Who's the 'Judge?' You mean these 'Witnesses' are just always watching us? What do you mean 'ready?' And *snatch* them up? What is this the mafia? What usually 'happens' to them? And what's going to happen to this guy that attacked me? I hope it's just hellish," he unloaded.

The nurse giggled at his madness and stern curiosity, "Well, let's see, so first, the Judge is pretty much the head honcho of the Town, you may have heard of him or seen him, he lives in that gargantuan white mansion on the mountainside. He's just a lonely, older gentleman. Humble guy, and *very* wealthy; I've even heard that he built and owns this whole Town! I've never met him or know anyone who has, I've only heard stories and rumors of what he's like—some good, some bad—,"

Peter cut her off again, "With all that money and being a loner I imagine he must not be a very pleasant guy," he hypothesized skeptically.

"Who knows, kid? Anyway, he's in charge, and the Town hasn't been *completely* destroyed yet," she joked. "Yeah, so these Witnesses they watch the people, and when they think that the people have had enough of their destructive lifestyles, they bring them before the Judge to give them a chance, I suppose, to do something better, I'm not entirely sure, to be honest. Everyone is different, though. They typically get brought in at a low, when they are more likely to accept, however, it's not forced; and some people might need to go through a little bit more than others to see if they are able to get out on their own."

Peter listened intently with deep interest.

"As far as what happens to the people that are brought in, I have very little knowledge of that, so I don't want to tell you an unintentional lie," finished the nurse.

"Hmm, this is all very interesting and new to me; how come he is such a reclusive mystery? Why doesn't he make himself known to the people, if he's supposedly 'taking care' of them?"

"No one knows."

"I'm not a fan. I don't like that; I want to meet this guy…so, where will they be taking that lunatic that tried to bludgeon me to death? Can I see the Judge there?"

"Bludgeon you to death?" squawked the nurse, "I thought he just jumped you and ran off?"

"Look, lady, this guy was rampaging after me, like a rabid wolverine! Can you imagine the ferocity? He was wild and crazy! I don't know what his intents were! He was coming for blood," Peter protested irrationally, but with a hint of an Andy-like smirk on his face.

The nurse snickered. "I'm starting to wonder which one of you was the real lunatic," she winked, "anyways, yeah he'll have a trial of sorts at the court."

Peter gave a puzzled look, "Where the devil would that be? I'm unaware of any sort of courthouse in this Town."

"It's only like a block west of that park with the biggest, oldest tree, you'd recognize it if you saw it."

"Okay, okay," he said, making silent plans in his head.

The nurse finished wrapping his arm in a cast and fastening the sling around his neck for his arm in which to rest, about which Peter had practically forgotten. "K, all done, sweetheart!"

"Oh, sweet!" said Peter acknowledging his arm, and hopping down from the patient table. As he headed for the door, he noticed the nurse was giving him a look of disappointment with her hands on her hips. In return, he said, "Oh, you did a great job on the cast, it looks really cool," with a snarky grin on his face, knowing what she was looking for, but not giving it to her; she remained with the same look and hands placed on her hips, only this time with raised eyebrows. Peter was still trying to act stubborn and angry, so he tried his hardest to play it cool, not admit defeat, and fight the urge to do anything nice, and remain a jerk; to remain in a state of depression, detestation and despair. He didn't *want* to be good. Once the tumult in his mind subsided, he looked her in the eye, said "Thanks," with a plain face, looked to the ground, and turned around, walking out the door.

Upon leaving the hospital, he had reason to feel uplifted after a humorous human exchange; not only from the pleasant conversation, but he also saw one of his favorite people running by: a man, who he named "Flip Flop" because he always wore flip flops, which he sees regularly—constantly running—and ordinarily always gets a laugh out of the sight of his funny run, along with a shirtless body. The combination thereof should have left him with a smile at least; but Peter chose to voluntarily shrug it off and slip back into his melancholy existence, pairing off with Ketten who was outside awaiting his company. "See, this is why I hate hospitals, they don't know what they're doing! I mean, what is the purpose of this?" Peter complained to Ketten, referring to the sling, and aiming his illogical anger at faultless targets.

Instead of wandering, and being led by Ketten, Peter led the way this time: they went straight to the courthouse (although previously unbeknownst to him). He was stubbornly absorbed in his pursuit to reveal this mysterious Judge character, and rashly lash out to a worthless outlet to receive some form of pleasant self-justice. He was so intensely engrossed, thinking about all the things he would (or just might get the chance to) say, that he almost didn't even notice the dog barking, growling and pausing at a certain point a ways back, appearing to not want to continue any further. When Peter looked back, he didn't care enough to endure Ketten's plea for his company any longer, and walked straight onward to his goal, Ketten veering off, disappeared into the streets. Peter went straight back to devising a dialogue, imagining the replies and the plethora of responses he would throw back in his face. He was angry, and felt like, perhaps, he had found a culprit for *all* his problems. He arrived at the courthouse and sat on the steps outside brewing a contentious stew of contempt in his head, while awaiting the trial.

When it appeared that the meeting was about to commence, Peter shuffled into the courtroom, with the rest of the congregation. He wondered if he was allowed to even be in there, but then recalled that he was a victim of one of the criminals, and justified his secretive appearance. The people, of whom the assembly was comprised, included what Peter assumed were the Witnesses, a few offenders of the citizens, and a bunch of random spectators, but no Judge. Peter attentively surveyed, awaiting the Judge's entrance. One of the Witnesses announced the Judge's entry and for the congregation to "all rise," Peter stood up anxiously to get a good look at his face. When the door opened and Peter saw the Judge's face, he was pounded with a tidal wave of unsettling, yet comfortable emotions. He was a bit perplexed to see the face of this man, and there was a calm sense of familiarity, beyond the fact that Peter *was* indeed familiar with this man: he was the unknown man in attendance at Andy's funeral, hence the perplexity. He was not expecting to have *this* man's face match the identity of the false perception of this Judge, which he had concocted in his mind. This angered Peter, fueling his meaningless blaming attacks. He had been in such disarray that when everyone else sat down, he was left standing with his facial expression resembling a plate of food tossed on the floor. He quickly took his seat soon thereafter in embarrassment. He had to pull himself repeatedly out of this distraction in order to observe the Judge's doings, as this was his intended purpose for joining the congregation.

His eyes and mind were open and clear, allowing an unbiased opinion to be formed, although thick clouds would frequently pass through, obstructing his perception. From what he'd observed of the conduct of the trial and even the setup of this courtroom, it differed from what he was used to seeing on TV, though he'd never been present for an actual trial. For example, the Judge either stood or sat at a desk that was unlike the elevated pedestal upon which normal judges sat; and as each offender was asked to stand before the Judge, he noticed the lack of any sort of lawyers to represent them. He carefully tried to pick apart the dialogue, the presentation of the incident and previous wrongdoings, the demeanor of both the Judge and defendant, essentially trying to find fault, all the while, in a state of denial of the fact that there were no apparent faults, but rather: simply *goodness*. Peter, recurrently, forcibly, shunted the noted opposition of his preconceived notions and belief of the deceit and malevolence of this man, leaving a pile of excuses dressed in resentment.

Peter honed in on the presentation of one of the defendants before the Judge. The Judge had explained what he did that brought him in here, as well as previous incidents. This particular defendant was extremely ashamed, staring at the floor. The Judge asked, "What are your feelings in regards to these actions and towards any victims?" Visibly crushed, this man couldn't get a word out. The Judge studied the man closely. The momentous silence was broken (and the man was lifted from the puddle into which he'd cried himself) by the Judge's verdict: "I think your penitence is evident," he said with a slow, wise tone in his voice, "I will pardon it. I will send you away with a charge to keep the law; you are free to go." He signed a paper, a Witness approached him, and they said a few things to each other—unheard from Peter's position—and the Witness escorted the man (who had a shocked smile on his face) as he thanked the Judge profusely, who smiled back at him. Peter was also in shock; he found his fault. He couldn't believe the Judge would so freely dismiss the man after hearing all the things he'd done. He instantly laid all the blame for his problems on the Judge, for *he* had been the one that allowed all the awful people of the Town to roam free, creating disorder and disrupting the peace, and, in Peter's case, inflicting personal harm. He couldn't help but feeling, however, deep down a sense of positive amazement regarding the verdict, and something else, perhaps a trace of jealousy. Though, he thrust it out of his mind, and stuck to his anger-doused heap of an obsession to prove his accusations right.

The truth is, Peter didn't know *what* to think or feel, but he continued watching this marvelously appalling scene. The next defendant was invited to stand before the

Judge. *This* man didn't seem ashamed rather he seemed irritated. None of the delinquents knew what to expect, they were brought there with very little to no knowledge and maybe some rumors of the results of these trials. In fact, most of them had expected to receive the fate that they had devised and convinced themselves of which they were worthy of deserving; most of which wasn't ever an attractive fate by any means, and on the other end of the spectrum, occasionally a fantasized easy trial where everything possible goes their way and more.

As the second defendant stood before the Judge to receive an unknown determination of the course of his life, Peter was curious to see what would happen. The same process took place: the reading off of past misdeeds (except this time the Judge was standing), he asked the same searching question, prompting the man's honest response. This time the man spoke, after a moment of pondering, "I don't really know. I mean, I'm sure the people I hurt or affected were upset and have unkind feelings towards me, but I had to fend for myself, if people get hurt in the process, that's not entirely my fault. Everyone's on their own in this life," defended the man. The Judge gave him a thick stare as his conscience worked out an outcome. He even stepped outside with one of the

Witnesses for a moment. Peter hated the secrecy and mystery. The Judge and Witness reentered, walked back to his desk, looked at the paper and then at the man, "I will pardon it. You are free to go with a charge to keep the law," he stated, signing the paper.

Peter was troubled. He started thinking up possible motives behind this Judge's strange behavior; for example, that maybe these people were only led to *believe* they were free, but were actually being sent to be exterminated in some inhumane fashion. However, that didn't add up or seem realistic, possible, but a long shot. He was extremely suspicious. This man was genuinely astounded, not in a grateful way, but more from a standpoint that this Judge must have been naïve, because he was off the hook, free to go back to his normal life, free from punishment or restriction. He was escorted out of the courtroom. There were only two remaining defendants, and it looked like Peter's attacker was going to be presented last.

The third man was brought up and underwent the exact same process; the only difference was the man. He was resilient in believing he was blameless in his self-inflicted victimization, and in callousness towards the Judge and everyone else in the room. He held a nasty look on his face and avoided any eye contact. This man had committed some relatively heinous crimes; many would contend that they were worse than the previous men's crimes, but they all did terrible things. The Judge thought deeply, and dissected the situation at hand, carefully putting together a worthy verdict. The Judge was meticulous and earnest in his work.

He concluded that this particular man needed something more eye opening. He sent him to be separated from society in a form of detainment he called "isolated conversion." This a treatment, where any and all who were subject to it would supposedly have a conversion of thoughts, ideas, beliefs, ultimately translating to a definite eventual complete change of actions through means of estrangement from everyone but themselves. There were different forms of isolated conversion. Some of which included actual isolated confinement with proper, regular care (food, etc.); others of which were not isolated, but rather the person was paired with one other person with which to live and cooperate, thus learning patience and compassion, or at least having such a desired outcome from said practice. Of course, one could argue that no one was ever truly alone, since the point of it was to be stuck with nothing but the thoughts of what they did to accompany them, which could only go two directions:

either one sulks and allows the negative feelings and actions to simmer and trigger more stirred up anger and animosity, or the one would be eaten alive by the guilt and plead for sweet release. However, beseeching alone out of pure anguish wouldn't necessarily be enough, there must be evident sincerity and true *conversion* of behavior; that's the goal. Again, this is more of a drastic measure taken strictly in certain circumstances, as determined by the Judge.

Peter was a little more comfortable with this verdict; it was surely fairer in his polluted eyes. He started to think that there was some sense in this Judge's mind. Peter hoped the same would happen to his perpetrator, if not something worse. He was called forth before the Judge, as his wrongs were stated and laid out before him. Peter's ears perked up when they mentioned his personal offense. The man gave his response to the Judge's question, at which Peter scoffed, deeming it fake. Peter awaited the words "isolated conversion" to fall out of the Judge's mouth. The silence seemed like years, when really after a few silent minutes, the Judge had his verdict. "I will pardon it, you are free to go, with a charge to keep the law, dismissed." Peter's jaw dropped; rather, it practically fell off his face, and shattered on the ground. Peter (silently) flew into a rage; he couldn't believe the "stupidity" of the Judge. The meeting was adjourned; the Judge stood and thanked everyone with a smile and left. Peter was too flustered to be able to do anything; his hesitation revoked from him the much-anticipated chance to confront the Judge.

After much contriving, Peter, being left nearly alone in the courtroom, approached a Witness and asked how he could speak with the Judge. The Witness said that for security purposes, he could not disclose his personal contact information, however the Judge is quite open to individual visits and would be glad to meet with him, then asked Peter's name. Peter was wary, and for a second thought about giving a fake name, but didn't. The Witness communicated that he was pleased to meet him and gave him his name. Peter was confused and critical of his cheerful attitude. He left feeling so frustrated. He laughed a little bit, not knowing what else to think or do. This Judge character was having a stronger impact on him than he'd like.

An infuriated Peter sat on the steps of the courthouse, where Ketten joined him, to ponder on this situation. "I can't believe he just let him go!" Peter objected to Ketten. He cycled through the possible reasons why this might make *any* sense in his mind. Doing so left him distracted from another process taking place in the deeper subconscious of his mind, of which he was unaware; past the surfacing frustrated attempts to accuse and condemn the Judge of his asinine verdicts, past the annoyance and pain of his healing arm, past the deeper bothersome relationship with the dog, past all that, deep at the root, on the path of his existence. We all walk a path of life; there are only two directions. Peter, up until this point, had been walking a dark path, baron, lifeless, and dismal. He thought there had to be something more. He kept coming back around, arriving at the ever-present and unclear detail that this *man* was crying at Andy's funeral, "why?" he kept thinking.

At this point in time, Peter, previously walking the dark path, stopped in his subconscious tracks, lifted his head up, looked around, as if just waking up, and turned his head to face what was behind him, gazing upon his footprints.

~ CHAPTER 7 ~

THE VICTORIOUS DEFEAT

Peter was walking alone at night. Wondering where Ketten was, he stood at intersecting streets, and looking to his left, he thought he saw Andy lying there in the street. He was suddenly brought to revisit Andy's funeral. Too difficult to watch, he turned away, and closed his eyes, then he remembered the Judge. Opening his eyes to try and get a better look at him, he saw that he was gone; in fact, no one was there.

Suddenly, transported to the courtroom, Peter was alone on one of the benches, after the trial had taken place, the Judge reentered, seeming very distant, he called out, "Peter."

The only thought that occupied his mind was "how does he know my name?"

The Judge looked at Peter and said, "I am waiting."

Peter looked muddled, "Waiting for what?"

The Judge just turned and left through the same door by which he entered.

"Wait! How do you know my name? What are you doing here?" asked Peter desperately, mustering a vague question to try and condense all of his concerns into one broad inquiry, so as to prompt an explanation from this enigmatic character. Feeling harassed, he lay his head down into his hand, covering his eyes. When he lifted his head, eyes open, he was back at the street.

He looked to the left, not seeing Andy, he thought it must all be in his head, and then he thought that his thoughts *are* all in his head, so what *is* really real? Once Peter was finished with his personal philosophical debate, he was enveloped by the almost tangible stillness of the air. Feeling the presence of a separate entity easing upon him from behind, he listened, ears perked. He heard breathing, as well as a faint tinkling sound. His eyebrows showing that he was indeed curiously puzzled by these shadowy noises, he slowly turned to identify them. As the image became clearer with increased perception from turning his head, his eyebrows raised to show utter disbelief and astonishment. He found Ketten. As Ketten slithered closer to Peter, coming into the light, Peter shrunk at the size to which the dog had grown and was apparently still growing. The dog had physically grown in size! Muscles visible and veins protruding, the dog (if you could even call it that anymore) stood, growling, making the meanest, vilest face. He had a massive hump on his shoulders, upon which rested chains, chains that wrapped around his body, and dangled to the ground (which explained the clinking sound). He stared Peter down with seemingly glowing red eyes, ears tucked back, the hair on his back standing up, baring his teeth and gums with what looked like blood dripping from the tips of his dagger-like fangs.

Peter was paralyzed, frozen with not even an inkling of what he could possibly do in this situation to evade any sort of pursuit, harm or demise. The formidable canine inched closer, and then paused. His apparent frenzied wrath had reached a boiling point and was now overflowing. He was generously enraged and hostile. He barked and lunged at Peter. Peter was able to nimbly dodge the attack and turn swiftly in the other direction to begin a sprint for his life. He never looked back, indeed, there was no need to; Ketten's barking and the clanking chains were a good enough indicator of how close he was behind him. Peter genuinely feared for his life at this moment. He was convinced there was a perilously real and inevitable certainty of his end. He knew he could no longer elude the dog's maneuvering, as his adrenaline supply would shortly be depleted, and full exhaustion would soon overcome his body; he also knew Ketten was relentless, and would not cease until he had claimed Peter's life. So, Peter concluded the "noble" thing to do would be to take it with honor, and fully accept the inescapable brutality that awaited him. He made a few brisk dodges and headed towards a spot with which he was familiar. Many thoughts rushed through his head in these brief moments, including firstly, the unexpectedness of the capabilities of power, which this being whom he had befriended possessed. Next, the thought or hope that he might reunite somehow with Andy graced his mind. Followed by a plethora of other random images and memories that embraced his mind. When Peter arrived at his designated spot, he stopped, and raised his arms upwards as if he was welcoming death, then one of his favorite songs began to play in his head, he looked up, and gave a faint smile, all of which seemed to happen in slow motion. He heard Ketten behind him approaching fast, the dog then leapt, mouth wide open, aiming to bite Peter at the neck. The dog's teeth made contact with his skin…abruptly, Peter awoke gasping for air. He found himself immediately curling into a fetal position, bracing for impact, clenching his whole body tightly. Tangled up in his bed sheets, he released his breath, and breathed in another deeply; then another, his muscles slowly relaxing.

He rubbed his eyes and lay atop the cushioning of his mattress with the discomfort of the bewilderment of what these scenes that his subconscious displayed meant. "Did I just die?" he thought out loud. His thoughts jumped to Ketten, replaying the common cycle of regret, second-guessing, and justification; he remained in fear of facing this problem, declaring it was beyond his control. Then he transferred to the Judge. "What *is* this man?" was the question in his mind. He resolved that he *needed* to meet this man, and conduct some sort of investigation to get to the bottom of his mound of concerns and find out what sort of misdeeds he was up to.

"Why am I so nervous?" said a frustrated Peter to himself in the mirror as he prepared himself to go meet the Judge. He headed out the door, a bit wary knowing that Ketten would likely show to accompany him. As he started making his way to the courthouse—taking a different route—he ran into Ketten, and was tremendously hesitant, anxious and frightened. He stood there staring at Ketten

flinching, awaiting for some attack; last night's
subconscious portrayal of the dog had left him petrified. "I
don't know if I want to be around you right now," he told
the dog. Ketten stood staring back at him with an intrigued
look. "Why don't you just leave?" said Peter with
trepidation. Ketten started walking away, but in the same
direction that Peter was heading. He waited a minute or
two watching as he casually and lightly trotted along the
walkway, sniffing parts of the grass. As Peter made his
way, he was vigilant of Ketten's every move, while Ketten
essentially stayed with him the whole way keeping a
substantial, yet mindful distance, however.

Peter made it to the courthouse, stared at the
entrance doors for a time, and then took a seat on the steps.
Suddenly, all the previous preplanned tactics to tear this
man down had been swept away; he had forgotten why he
was there. He had to re-convince himself to do it, and
remind himself of his intentions. Once he had again gained
loyalty to his own antagonistic devices, he eagerly entered
the courthouse looking for the Judge. He asked a Witness,
who relayed that a trial was in session. He was curious to
see if this trial would resemble the one, which he sat in on,
but when he tried to open the door to sneak in, it was
locked. He found a chair nearby and took a seat to wait for

the end of the trial. His thoughts became scattered again, so he had to compile them once more.

A Witness came and asked if he needed any help.

"No I'm good," Peter said, giving him a look of irritation that he was disrupting his train of thought.

The trial ended and Peter stood up apprehensively, watched as the attendants flooded out the doors, until it became a trickle, once it seemed like the flow of people had stopped, he entered the courtroom hoping to have a one-on-one confrontation with the Judge. When he got inside the room it was empty, he must have just missed him. He sat down on of the benches, and rested his head in his hands.

Several minutes passed before the Judge reentered the room, "Peter," he called out.

Peter's head shot up; this instance struck a familiar chord, and he was in awe, and a little alarmed. He watchfully waited for the next words that would come out of the Judge's mouth.

"Need some help?" the Judge teased with a grin.

Peter, now regaining a grip on the reality of the situation, eased out of his deer-in-headlights position, gave a slight sigh of relief, as he was not sure if he was ready to deal with that sort of insanity, had it been a duplicate of his previous nighttime visitation. He blinked a few times, shook his head and then when it finally registered that the Judge somehow knew his name, he asked, "How do you know my name?"

"I guessed?" said the grinning Judge, portraying a slight undertone of humor. "Now, Peter, which do you prefer: fruit tea, hot chocolate, or just water?"

Peter, tortured by the insignificance of this request, was utterly dumbfounded, and the odd question only fed his predisposed idea that this Judge was idiotically oblivious, "What does that have to do with *anything*!" he angrily retorted.

"I wanted to invite you to my house, so that we may discuss your concerns, and I planned on providing a beverage" said the Judge.

Peter's brain was firing off in all sorts of directions. His suspicion peaked, nevertheless he accepted the invitation, "But I'll have chocolate milk; if that's okay with you," he insisted, peering at him.

"Excellent! Tomorrow at 4, and I believe you know where it is that I live, am I correct?" asked the Judge.

"Yep, I'll be there," he replied with a tone that discretely exposed his standpoint of enmity towards him.

Peter was left with such a disoriented feeling, unknowing of what had just now taken place, and to what he had agreed. He went home rather distraught and began imagining all types of heinous things that could happen at this meeting.

The next day, he tensely travelled to the Judge's great white mansion on the hillside. He knocked on the door.

"Peter! Come on in!" the Judge welcomed.

Still looking at him, not giving the expected reactions to such niceties, with mistrust, Peter asked, "Do I need to take my shoes off?"

"Nonsense, there's no need for that."

Peter was curious, noting that his demeanor was much different outside of a courtroom setting.

"So, Peter, I have your chocolate milk ready, I also have some hot apple cider, as well as orange juice. Oh! I also have crackers."

Peter was impressed with his generosity, however, declined to express his thankfulness, which was difficult—he loves crackers. He carefully inspected his house.

"Peter, why don't you take a seat, here," the Judge insisted.

Peter obliged. He continued to inspect, while the Judge prepared a few last things in the kitchen. Peter's intention was to mainly observe and try to catch him in anything he might say that seemed "off," and to not allow much dialogue from his end.

The Judge entered and sat in a chair diagonally across from Peter, crossed his legs and took a sip from his mug, looked at the floor, looked at Peter, smiled, and said "Now, Peter, I know you're wondering why I've invited you personally to my residence," he paused, set down his mug, while searching Peter's expression, "I've seen it enough to know when someone is upset with my, '*work*,' we'll call it. Many people have requested my company, so as to relinquish the often maniacal, deliberate and outright disapproval and detestation of what I'd done. Peter, I believe you're in a similar position, so, you may '*unleash*,'" he smiled and put his interwoven fingers up to his mouth, resting his chin on his thumbs.

Peter, in attempt to not give the Judge the privilege of being right, hurriedly and flustered, came up with an alternate excuse for his requesting a voice with the Judge, "Oh, well that's wild and crazy, but actually I wanted to find out more about what a man of your position does. I was curious, so I came to a trial, and I am just so interested in what judges do," he replied with an innocent smile.

"Oh, ahem, okay, I apologize for assuming,"

Peter laughed an evil laugh in his head.

"I love talking about what I do! Well, you see, it is imperative that you understand preeminently how I receive my information. My team of Witnesses does just that, they 'witness' the goings-on of the people of this lovely Town, and they bring people to me when they've driven themselves straight into the slums, thus, they watch when people are getting to that point, they record who is involved in their misdeeds, and they relay all the details to me, so that I, as a Judge, can give an apt verdict."

At this point Peter, was starting to become nervous, as he was putting the pieces together, that the Judge still knows—somehow—plenty about him and his intents.

"So, as you can tell, I know a lot about a lot of people here in Town," the Judge described with a smile.

"Peter, you and I both know why you are truly here," said the Judge, with a victorious grin.

Peter sat motionless, not even blinking, as if he believed motionlessness was a common tactic of avoiding detection much like when confronted by a Tyrannosaurus

Rex; it proved futile. "Yeah, alright, I'm really quite angry with your decision to let that man go!" Peter confessed after succumbing. He paused, looking at the Judge as if waiting for response or permission.

The Judge motioned by nodding for Peter to continue.

"I just feel like it is completely absurd that this Town is overrun with thugs, criminals and lunatics! I feel that…the fault is yours for all of the chaos, and *stupid* people that are just toxic *parasites* amongst all of us trying to live a normal life! I've had to deal with so much crap; you have no idea! They killed my best friend, Andy, did you know about that? What happened to *those* guys? You said this town was 'lovely,' now I would like to know how in the *world* you could ever come to such an *asinine* conclusion! I am just not comprehending how you, as a judge, can sit here and tell me that this Town is 'lovely' and that everything is just fine, and that there is 'justice.' I've had so much wrong done to me, so many things stolen, never returned, and never anything good to compensate for the bad. Tell me how is that *just*? I've had nothing but the nastiest of *trash* dealt to me, just pure garbage of a life. I don't have anyone now, I don't even know if I could have anyone else; no one talks to me, *especially* not girls! I bet you can't even relate, you probably have no idea what the people of this Town go through, do you? You have this nice, quiet, voluptuous mansion all to yourself. You don't know pain. You don't know poverty. Who gave you the right to be here, to do what you do? You've sure done a bang-up job *ruining* this Town. You've sure ruined *my* life. Oh, and are you responsible for the highly trained dog that has been wasting my life away too, that has latched on like a leech? The list goes on and on. I *hate* this place! I didn't sign up for this! Also, if the Town is so bad, and so many people have complained about it, then why haven't you done anything to fix it? What happened to all those people and their complaints?"

Peter had started out hesitant, then released all the pent up aggression and accusations, until he was almost at a loss of words because he was so flustered, and he didn't know where to begin again. As he began, however, all of his hostile attacks spilled out at once, ending up as an unpleasant mess on the floor. The more he gave in to unleashing his anger, he became paradoxically more angry, coming up with new excuses to crucify this figure and all of his "ill-used power."

All the while, the Judge sat and listened, and studied Peter, looking for something more, something deeper. When Peter had mentioned the dog, the Judge's ears perked up, as if he found something.

"I just don't want to deal with this anymore!" Peter added finally.

The Judge took a deep breath, and made sure Peter was finished, when it seemed so, he said, "Well, Peter, that's your prerogative," with a subtle smile.

Peter returned a look that replicated as though he thought the Judge was the biggest idiot, mixed with a bit of a face of constipation; in other words, Peter was utterly stupefied. "What?" he said with a tone that reflected the same emotions as his facial expressions.

"Simple as that," the Judge established.

Peter sneered.

"Peter, do you *have* to be here?"

"What does that even mean?" he answered sharply.

"What brought you here?" the Judge asked a follow-up question.

"Why do you always do that? You ask irrelevant questions, that are completely off-topic and avoid the subject," Peter said observantly.

"It was your choice," said the Judge, ignoring Peter's ranting.

"Excuse me?" said Peter, half-hearing what he said, but also intentionally not listening.

"Your *choice*, Peter," repeated the Judge.

Peter tried to come back, "Wh—," he stopped, and stayed about as still as a paused frame of a film, his tongue seized mid-word, unable to speak. He evidently understood, and was caught up in an epiphany.

"You see, Peter, I am not responsible for anything, no one forces you to cause any of that, which is placed before you, to be of detriment to you, as it has."

Peter was sobered, but he could not allow himself to let the Judge gain a victory. His face remained expressionless, while inside a battle raged.

"Now, Peter, tell me about this *dog*."

Peter was urged to respond in a harsh manner, but instead replied with humility, "Well, it's been following me for years—or rather I've been following *him*, I don't really know. I never could have imagine it would become such a 'ball and chain.' He's got pointy ears, dark brown hair mixed with some black, a collar with a tag that only says 'Ketten,' which I assumed was his name, at least that's what I call him."

"Hmm…and where do you follow him?"

Peter sighed a sigh of submission to this apparent disclosure of events kept secret for years, "Well, I don't know. We just walk around the Town, but almost every night, I see parts of the Town that I've never seen before," he said with reflection and seeming *disgust* with some of the memories of places he'd seen, he continued, "and I lose track of time, and of where we're at and then when I come to my senses, I feel *drained* and ill and I just want to leave."

The Judge was curious how it was affecting Peter.

"But at the same time, I am always so curious where it will lead me and it's almost, calming? I can't think of a better word, but I don't really see anything *wrong* with it."

"*What* is it 'calming,' Peter?" asked the Judge, with investigative eyes.

Peter, displeased with this sense of an interrogation, didn't give a straight answer, "I don't know!" he snapped, "My life sucks! It's an escape, I feel like no one else understands, or accepts me fully, but I can at least talk openly with him and I feel like that helps me."

"Tell me, when do you see…Ketten, is it? When do you usually see him?" probed the Judge.

"Aha! So you *do* have something to do with him!"

The Judge was puzzled.

"How did you know his name?" Peter attacked, confident that he had caught him in his lie.

"Peter, you are being nonsensical, you just *told* me his name not two minutes ago," defended the Judge calmly and with a smile.

"Oh. Right." Peter accepted with blushed cheeks.

The Judge gawked at him with raised eyebrows awaiting the answer to his previous question.

"Yeah, so I don't really know the answer to your question. I see him all the time, I don't know what else you want to know."

"What I want to know, Peter, is *why* you are going to Ketten. I've seen similar things to this before, and as I understand, there is always an underlying, causal origin of such patterns of behavior. I want to help, Peter," consoled the Judge.

"Help what, Judge? As far as I'm concerned there's nothing to be helped! I don't need your help," retorted Peter stubbornly, as he gathered himself and his things to leave. He made for the door.

The Judge allowed him to leave, but called out, "Don't not come back!"

"Thanks for the crackers!" Peter replied and slammed the door on his way out. He was very ruffled and confronted with anxiety. His hardened heart would not permit the Judge's penetrating questions to continue, for deep down he knew where that leads, and such grand change is not something he wants to take on at this time.

As Peter walked home, there was a stew of negative thoughts brewing. Although, as he came upon a fast food burger joint, which he'd learned to detest through a few too many stomachaches, he witnessed the "parasitic, systematic machinery of a society tethered to the industry of substance, shackled to ease and illusion," by which he has become repulsed, of course he favors a rather extreme set of views on some things, but this time it struck him. Peter began to ponder. Was *he* a victim of such a lifestyle? A cog in the machine, which he hated? A slave to another entity? Such were his thoughts, which prompted the contemplation of whether or not he should abandon Ketten or let it be. Perhaps it was time to surrender. Peter was stumped as to what this surrender would mean.

~ CHAPTER 8 ~

CONTRITION

The Judge sat in the same chair after Peter left, pondering for more than an hour. He thought deeply about the small bits of information that Peter dispensed, but he assessed all of the other hints that he may have dropped by the tone of his voice, or body language, etc. He was trying to learn Peter.

Peter, on his way home, ran into a familiar face, which he was glad to see. It was the face of James.

"Hey, buddy! How you doin'?" James said.

"Hey, James, I'm doing satisfactory. What are you doing?" replied Peter; unsure of the answer he gave.

"Good, dude. Oh yeah, I'm just heading back from class, I was going to grab something to eat; you wanna join me?"

Peter hesitated, since he had a lot going through his mind, which he didn't really want to interrupt. He was basically a scavenger, anytime there was even a chance of free food, wherever it may be, under whatever circumstances the free food was being given out, he was there, so it was surprising that he didn't immediately pounce on the offer. However, after a little consideration, he finally agreed, "Only if it's tacos or pizza," he said jokingly, also hoping this coincidental encounter could possibly be of some help.

Peter was in a better mood now that he was with James. It had been a long while since they'd seen each other. Peter was taking advantage of this distraction from his present matter by not focusing on any one subject or giving an update how things are going for him, because he didn't really want to open up, knowing that it would require a longer, deeper discussion, and he wasn't sure how personal he wanted to get with James. Although, he would like to get some feedback; for that is the type of person Peter is, he likes to talk, to display his thoughts in the form of words, and then determine how crazy he is or is not based on how they are received. Meanwhile, as they took their seat in the restaurant, he let his random exaggeratory imagination run wild, putting off the real discussion for a little later by saying things like: "What if your name was just 'Jame?' You could just claim that you have a phobia of plurals. And when you get scared you would say 'yike!' And you would wear 'pant,' and cut paper with 'scissor.'"

James was a fan of that one.

"When I have a son I'm going to name him Earl, but I'm just going to spell it 'R-l.' Yep, Rl Fischer. Ya know, I just want to be cool like those people who name their kid Alex, but spell it all wack like: 'A-a-l-e-k-s-x-h,' or something egregious like that, the second 'a' and 'xh' are silent," Peter quipped, and they laughed some more.

Suddenly James' laughter ceased as he was evidently captivated by something behind Peter.

Peter investigated what was the cause of such abrupt change in composure; when he turned to look, he too was stunned. "Oh, who's that Jamesy boy?" pried Peter with a massive grin on his face.

"She's gorgeous," answered James, wearing a sappy smile and red cheeks.

"I didn't know you had a lady friend, when are you guys getting married?" teased Peter.

"Shut up!" James chuckled, "I've never even spoke to her."

"What's this beaut's name? She's truly a peach!" said Peter, winking, "I need to find me a fresh hunny like that though, for real. Where do you find 'em?"

"Her name is Isabelle Fairchild, and I love her. Just kidding, I don't know anything about her, except that she loves pandas…and, my friend, you have to first acquire the devilishly good looks that I possess in order to woo the ladies, then they will swoon, and you'll be a modern-day hero among men."

"Oh, Jameson, I didn't know you were the stalker type! Fairchild, eh? She is one 'fair child.' And please tell me how I can acquire these paralyzing good looks of which you speak!"

They joked a bit more, and then Isabelle came over to their table to check on them, smiling of course, as that is part of her job.

"Goodness me, did you see that smile she threw your way? Jeez, do you guys have any names picked out for your children?" Peter teased once she left, "I'm no expert, but I'm *pretty* certain that means she wants you to propose to her right now."

James was sort of half listening, so he gave a slight chuckle, but was mostly enthralled and in a stupor, with a bright red face.

Peter laughed at him, and then was suddenly, randomly reminded of his predicament, and became occupied with the overwhelming task of identifying a solution, as well as the causes. His eyes stared down at the saltshaker on the table, but it was clear that he was seeing something entirely different.

James noticed and asked with a smirk, "What's wrong, dude, you jealous?" thus catalyzing the *serious* part of their discussion.

"Nah, dude I'm just thinking about all the stuff I got going on right now."

"Like what, man?" Does it have anything to do with Andy?" he suggested.

"Well, I just think that's always going to be a problem, I'm always going to be wrecked because of that. No, it's about other things," said Peter hesitantly, not completely sure if he wanted to tell James about his private problem.

"Oh, well, I know how hard it's been with losing Andy, but I believe things will be alright, it's just up to you. And you don't gotta tell me about your other stuff if you don't want to."

Peter ignored the bit of advice pertaining to Andy because he didn't agree with it, and decided he'd divulge his secret, "Nah, it's fine, I can tell you. I have this *problem*, I can't seem to get rid of. There's this dog that has been following me around, or me him, I don't know, but it's been going on for years now. It's really been kind of weighing me down."

James gave him a look as if he was waiting for something else a little more *shocking* or serious, but hiding the confusion behind a concerned face. However, he could not successfully hold back the urge to laugh, "That's it, just a dog?" he said, lovingly taunting Peter.

"Hmm...I guess that does kind of beg more context. It does sound rather pitiful and absurd," he acknowledged, giving a tiny self-conscious chuckle, then continuing. "Okay, so it *is* a dog, if not some sort of demon beast that is in the *form* of a dog. I first encountered it with Andy, when we were rummaging through an abandoned car. I was curious. He didn't act like a typical dog, but he kept showing up so I just kept hanging around him. Then just as the years have gone by, he's become angrier and, I guess more *clingy* or attached. He gets angry if I don't feed him, and when I feed him too, he gets really snappy and greedy. It's like I can't win, the more I do really *anything* he backs me further into a corner. But I guess he's not really doing any harm; I mean he hasn't killed anybody, that I know of at least; that could be untrue for all I know. He *has* killed a lot of birds…I love birds," he explained simply, mourning over the birds.

"Well, that doesn't sound like a true friend. I mean, did Andy ever go around killing things you love."

Peter gave him a sympathy smirk stamped on a look of disapproval of his witticism.

"I'm just sayin', it doesn't sound to me like someone, or something you'd want to keep around. But for reals Pete, it doesn't sound all that great, and as far as him not doing any harm, I think that may just be *your* perception, either that, or your rationalization. I mean, I will say honestly I do sense a difference in you. You *do* seem like distraught in some way; besides the fact that I now know that you are in fact dealing with something that is *causing* said distress. I know it doesn't really say much, but I've known you a long time, and when you and Andy used to play when you guys were younger, you always seemed so carefree. Like I said, that doesn't say much, because when you're young, you usually are much more carefree, so I don't have much to compare how you 'normally' are or are not at *this* stage in your life," assessed James.

Peter accepted this evaluation. It struck him. However, he wasn't quite sure what to make of it; he knew something hit him but he didn't know what it was, almost like it wasn't time for him to understand it, but there was something of import about what James said. "Wow. Alright…you know you're a real grade-A guy," he added admiringly. His appreciation was more directed at how kind James has been to Peter all these years, however. He was still hesitant regarding his advice on Ketten and himself, for he doesn't like being told what to do. Despite that, he trusts James, but as he was talking Peter reflected on how great he is, and became occupied with this train of thought, while still listening. "Really though, man, thanks for being like an older brother to *me*. And it seems like you've been doing well handling the whole Andy thing. I really look up to you, man. And that crap's not easy for me to say, so you better take that compliment with so much appreciation!" he said, laughing at his own sarcasm. With that compliment, he also successfully diverted a further discussion of the topic.

James laughed and accepted the compliment with much gratitude, "I know, I know. I am already aware of how great I am," he laughed some more, "Nah, just kiddin' dude. Thanks buddy, that means a lot. I hope all goes well with you and you can figure out whatever it is you need to figure out. If you need anything, just let me know, k bro? Serious."

"Alright, man, well, should we head out?"

"Yeah"

As they started to get everything together to leave, Peter said, "I feel like I'm forgetting something," so as to stall James from leaving, then looked at him smugly, and suddenly turned around and yelled, "Hey Isabelle!" then turned around and ducked his head.

When she turned in the direction from which she heard her name, all she saw was James giving her a deer-in-headlights look, while Peter giggled like a schoolchild.

"Peter! What the devil?" James whispered angrily at Peter, which only provoked more giggling.

She finished up what she was doing at another table, and then came over to James and Peter's table, "Yes?" she inquired.

"Oh yes, sorry about that, it was just my friend here, he can be a real turd sometimes. You see, he's special needs, and I take care of him. I'm his caretaker." James explained, smiling really big at Isabelle.

Peter gave him an insulted look, but still thought it was hilarious.

She looked at him and said "Aw, that is *so* sweet!" Then turning to Peter, asked, "What's his name?"

"Peter," James told her.

"Hi, Peter! How are you?" she said sticking out her hand for a handshake.

Peter acted very bashful, still giggling.

"He likes high-fives," said James.

She gave him a high-five, "Oh, you are adorable!" she said and then gave him a hug.

Peter's face lit up.

James shook his head at Peter with jealousy.

Isabelle looked back at James, "Do we know each other?"

"Uh, yeah. Well, no, not officially I suppose. We're in a class together. It's quite a coincidence to see you working here. My name's James," he extended his hand.

She shook it, "Oh, well it's nice to officially meet you. I guess you already know *my* name," she said pointing to her nametag.

They both laughed.

Just then Peter handed her a napkin that he had written on, "Here," he said loudly.

"Oh, what's this?" she said curiously.

He pointed at James.

She showed it to him.

He was surprised to see his phone number written down. "Oh, that's, my number, he has a good memory with numbers," he said blushing.

Isabelle blushed as well.

Peter giggled.

"Well, we're going to be heading out now, it was nice talking to you and the food was delectable. I guess I'll see you around," said James.

"Likewise!" Isabelle said with a smile. She said goodbye to both of them and they left.

As soon as they stepped outside, Peter burst out laughing.

James gave an annoyed laugh.

"Special needs, eh?" You're such an idiot! So, now that you guys have a wedding date planned, what are you going to do about me? You don't want the foundation of your marriage to be based on a lie do you?" Peter teased.

"Well, you *do* play the part well," was James' comeback, "I can't believe you did that, you little pecker!" he said both frustrated because of his embarrassment, and exhilarated because the girl whom he has a huge crush on has his number and knows his name.

"What? You should be *thanking* me!"

"I know, I'm pretty stoked, but you're still a twit," said James cheerfully but spitefully.

They teased each other a bit more, and then James had to head off so they said goodbye and split ways.

Almost instantly once Peter was in solitude, his laughter gave way to a serious demeanor as James' advice came to mind unexpectedly. He figured this would keep himself occupied on the way home.

He was bothered by it, but he didn't quite know why. So, on the way, Peter sat back, while the two parts, two opposing sides of his mind debated the topic. He went back and forth between believing James was an inspired man and believing that he was completely ignorant. On the one hand, James has no idea or comprehension of the *scale* of his quandary, thus Peter would argue that it really was worse than it sounds in words. On the other hand, James is a trusted friend of Peter's and knows him well, thus Peter would argue that if he sees a noticeable difference, then it may be worth giving a deeper look. All of such conclusions helped Peter to see that his *problem* was indeed real and, just as he argued, it *was* worse than it sounded, and in need of resolution; something perhaps he hadn't quite fully accepted. These realizations opened a floodgate of deeper insight and recognitions, but Peter dammed the flow before he could receive the full amount, however, it was enough to *see* with sufficient clarity. Peter was struck by the fact that there was an apparent difference in his countenance (he took James at his word on that).

Perhaps it *had* been doing harm all these years, not detrimentally all at once, but gradually—little by little. (With each new insight gained, he saw deeper and clearer, as if they built off of each other), His thoughts kept progressing: maybe it's hard for him to distinguish the harm because that's the most prevalent thing he sees when he looks back—that's the only life he knows, at least on the surface. He regretted that he was apparently not the person he could be. "I'm not *me,*" he said out loud. He observed, perhaps for the first time, that he was affected by the presence of this dog, evidently physically— outwardly—as well as mentally and emotionally of course, since his anger, fear, depression, and anxiety were heightened. He was pained by the thought of the relationships he had possibly damaged because of this mental infection, or even worse: the relationships he had inhibited himself from having due to this. He thought back to his recent discovery, that he had become that, which he had viewed in disgust—the slaves of substance. He saw how *he* was employing a substance in order to have peace, but it was a false, illusory peace. He is a slave. He felt imprisoned, broken, bound, helpless, and lost. He felt as if darkness and light were having a tug of war and he was the rope; he was being torn apart.

~ CHAPTER 9 ~

THE NEW CHAPTER

As Peter unlocked this newfound remorse for what he had become—and all because he had become hooked to this entity—Peter was confronted by the very beast he just learned he must conquer. His heart began pumping violently as he stared at Ketten, wondering what would follow. His mind slipped into a subconscious state of the possible proceedings, meanwhile, it seemed as though time paused. He stepped back and weighed the options. His rationalization took him in a circle beginning with how the dog's appearance was very "convenient," and that since he had been just now realizing how much Ketten had gotten a hold of him, he should probably choose to stop joining with him—he wondered what it would be like, to not feel controlled by him, tethered by fear. Then he thought about how it's not really *that* bad, he can still manage life just fine with this extra load. The next thought was that perhaps *now* that he has these novel comprehensions, maybe he could tag along with Ketten—with open eyes this time, assuming this gave him some sort of immunity—and spot the effect that he has on him. Unfortunately his thought process didn't make a full revolution back to where he started, and he decided that it was reasonable to choose to accompany Ketten at this time.

When he came to—or time resumed—he noticed Ketten possessed an absolutely horrendous guise, directed at Peter. The hair on his back was standing up, his eyes appeared red, ears laid back, tail down, bearing his teeth, hunched over; Peter felt real fear. He then confidently said, "Hey, would you calm down, I'm coming with you." That still didn't satisfy Ketten, for nothing really satisfies this dog, nevertheless, he turned and started on his path, urging Peter to follow, as usual. They proceeded. Peter was ever curious, as well as—with his newly opened eyes— adamant about wrapping his head around this affliction.

Peter was vigilant in attempting to identify what it was that drew him to Ketten—the root causation of his continuous return to him—and the damage he had sustained in keeping him around. He tried to talk himself through the recent revelations that came to him, he wanted to be sure of himself and fully convinced that he was involuntarily bound. He simultaneously tried to learn

Ketten as well as keep these items on his mental list straight, however, such a task proved to be overwhelming for Peter, especially since the trancelike state—the numb unconsciousness, the lack of ability to decipher and decide—that usually occurs when following Ketten, had begun to settle in. These thoughts were slowly weeded out as Ketten seduced Peter, until he was lost in an abyss, only a blurry awareness as his sight. It had been a substantial amount of time, before one could find Peter sitting on a curb, in a blankness, looking as though his mind was vacant, his eyes open although unresponsive and rolling back into his skull every few minutes. Suddenly Peter blinked and consciously began to perceive his surrounds; it was dark, he was in an unfamiliar alleyway, Ketten was absent. "Why?" he muttered to himself. He started to pick himself up, and Ketten came around the corner, alert to what Peter was planning. He was still groggy as if he'd just woken up, but looked closer and saw that Ketten had blood all over his mouth, "What in the world! What are you doing?" he exclaimed. The dog turned back and went around the corner from where he came, unentertained by Peter's displeasure. Peter didn't know if he dared to look, he hesitated for a moment before his aching curiosity dragged him around the corner. Peter saw something he wished he hadn't. Ketten had killed a dog and was feeding on the carcass.

Peter's heart dropped and he covered his mouth in shock with his hand. He rolled over around the corner against the wall, out of sight of the dog, and shed a tear. He contemplated bolting away—far away—but part of his mind argued against it giving heed to and fearing the *base* display, which he had just now witnessed. Just as he was about to make his split decision, Ketten barked the most ferocious bark Peter had ever heard. He hesitated to turn the corner again to face him, but it was too late, he felt his presence next to him, he looked down to behold Ketten's savagery and seeming growth in size and destructive capabilities. He held his breath as they stared at one another, Peter waiting in agony to see what would await him, his mind shifted into another abyssal plane of focus that included only the two of them. It was as if Peter was interviewing Ketten, pleading to figure out what the dog wanted from him, desperately trying to determine what his purpose and intent was. Unable to find an answer, Peter came back and released the breath he was holding, and asked calmly, "Okay, what?" flinching, prepared to defend himself to the best of his human ability. He closed his eyes, and when he again opened them to see what he was doing, he saw that he had already started on his path, and turned to urge Peter by growling and barking until he advanced. Peter succumbed. He remembered his original mission and thought he could still gather some valuable bits of information.

Peter was able to remain aware this time, free from being arrested by Ketten's cryptic hypnotic abilities. Though watchful, Peter's efforts in tracing his engagement with this creature to a viable root destination were still fruitless. Until a few moments passed and Ketten stopped, Peter, caught off guard, looked around. Completely unfamiliar with the area, He became concerned; he felt something looming. The place where they had arrived looked very surreal; he was unaware that parts like this existed in this Town. He wondered for a second if they had somehow, unbeknownst to him, travelled outside of their Town. Peter watched carefully as Ketten seemed to have calmed down, as if he were preparing for something. Ketten slowly walked around the corner after looking at Peter like he was summoning him. Peter stood, staring. He noticed that Ketten wasn't coming back, nor barking at him, as Ketten typically made every effort to not loose his grasp on Peter. He wondered—even began to fantasize about the implication—if Ketten had vanished, for good.

"Is he gone?" he asked himself aloud. Peter crept over to the corner, full of angst, and a shred of hopefulness. Everything seemed to be moving in slow motion. As Peter rounded the corner, he became subject to an onslaught of a foulness of a degree, which he had never before experienced. He was simply astounded. Horrified and fearful, he wanted to look away, but felt he couldn't for how disturbingly shocking it was. He tried to take it all in, to perceive if it were indeed reality or not. Peter was in utter disbelief; and there stood Ketten, wagging his tail in front of it all.

A few days had passed and Peter was still trying to pick up the pieces of his mind that had been shattered by the display of such gross proportions, which he had recently beheld. He could not comprehend it. He saw *something,* which, he felt, destroyed him. He was still a little numb, unsure of what to make of it. He cringed, his face twitching, as thoughts and images were called back spontaneously to him. He knew, somewhere in his mind, that he needed to keep himself away from the atrocity called Ketten, but to do so, he knew it would be grueling. He knew he couldn't do it alone, nor would he want to if he would undertake this task. This process would require *his* full understanding of his problem, and his full understanding included a disclosure and discussion with a sober-minded person (as he learned best by talking things out), which thought fed his fear, for it is not something he would like to discuss, let alone did he know with whom he could, the possibility was muddled in the cloud of chaos swirling in his brain. Surely he knew there were pieces of the sense to be made of this floating about, but he could not grab hold of them. Suddenly, the Judge popped into his mind. He was unconvinced that he would be the man for the job. As he walked around aimlessly, the thoughts cycling through his mind, the Judge kept coming up; it was not a very strong impression, and Peter became increasingly annoyed with it. Until finally he accepted the impression and chose at some point in the coming days he would contact the Judge to speak with him, he accepted begrudgingly, but he accepted.

Another week expired, and Peter still hadn't followed through with his stubborn commitment. Until the day he woke up from another dream where Ketten was attacking, intent on killing him. He determined he'd finally seek the Judge's counsel. He was resolute to rid himself of the cancer that had overcome him. He got himself ready

and headed over straightway to the Judge's place. When
he arrived out front, he began pacing around on the porch,
trying to compose his thoughts. Unbeknownst to Peter, the
Judge had noticed, and was observing, his arrival and
nervous pacing. Peter's efforts to gather and organize his
thoughts were futile. Flustered, he went up to the door to
knock; he only got one knock in before the Judge
immediately opened the door, giving Peter a nice, warm
smile, like he was glad to see him. Peter was startled at his
promptness. He stepped aside and motioned for Peter to
enter. "What, were you watching me or something?" said
Peter as he walked inside.

"I must shamefully admit affirmatively to that, but
in my defense, my first thought was that you were here to
vandalize my property," he said chuckling lightly.

"Oh yeah? Well, why do you care? It's not like
you don't have enough money to repair your *voluptuous*
mansion," he said bluntly while heading straight for the
chair in which he sat during his previous visit, "you know,
you still never explained that," he said taking his seat.

The Judge jumped straight into answering, "Peter,
when I first came here, I was very, very wealthy. With
time, and the more I gave to the Town, I ended up losing
everything. When I could no longer pay for this house,

some of the people of the Town, with whom I worked closely suggested that I remain the owner and continue living here, for it's not obstructing anything, no one else would be able to pay for it, nor was there any use tearing it down; in other words it would otherwise just be empty and abandoned and rot over time," he explained frankly and confidently.

Peter was struck by the fact that the Judge claimed to have generously given so much to the people of the Town; he stored that in the back of his mind for later, as it might be of some import.

"Of course, I still try to give as much as I can to the Town, and not just financially," added the Judge delightfully while Peter was thinking. The Judge imposed before Peter could whip out the assortment of possible pointless (in the eyes of the Judge) counter questions, "But that's not why you have come today, is it, Peter?" he prodded.

Peter was okay with that for now. He looked down, "Yeah, it's Ketten." In deep humility, Peter looked to the Judge to accept his previously rejected offer of help. Peter looked up, expecting the Judge to say something, but he sat quietly, open and ready to hear from Peter, eager to help. That was enough for Peter; he didn't need a cue to talk, "So I've realized some things about this dog and, I think, his intents. By the way, prepare yourself, because this is going to be all over the place, like 'word vomit,'"

The Judge just nodded.

"So, the other day, I decided to follow Ketten after he ironically showed up, because I felt that *this* time I could keep an open mind and *catch* him, ya know? Because I had just had some enlightening realizations like right before he appeared. For example, I saw how he was truly imprisoning me. He controls me! But I saw how *I* was using him as an escape; he is my 'substance.' It just made me forget about everything that I was worrying about. I could *fly away* for those moments. But, I think it was a false sense of calm. Yeah, and I was just lead further and further to believe that it was solving things, but really I was just being more and more hindered. Man, how the bloody devil did I get to this point? Lies. Monstrous lies. I'm just a freaking bum. A piece of crap. But, it was so gradual. I was curious, and then all of a sudden, he was latched on, incising little by little each time I saw him, until he crawled under my skin, and sunk into my brain and made his home there. He just slowly infected and corrupted me; I am angry all the time. Stubborn and rebellious, what is the meaning of this mutiny? If I could have seen the beginning from the end, side by side, I would surely refuse as if I were being offered feces on a plate to eat. But, of course that's the only way he could have gotten a hold of me like he has…gradually."

Peter was finding out new things as he unloaded. He stopped talking for a moment to let it all settle, staring at the carpet. The Judge remained silent and attentive. "I didn't sign up for this! I just want to be freed from this enslavement. But I have no idea *how*, I mean any time I try to do *anything*, *especially* try to get away from him, he's there and waiting to take me away, and displays his anger with my desires to remove myself from him. It's easy to go back to him. I can't possibly separate from him. I don't see that happening. There's nothing I can do. I'll just have to wait till he like dies or something," he said with a look of hopelessness, "I just feel so crippled. It's very debilitating, the fear, I've been conditioned and blinded. I'm afraid, to let go. I don't know what would happen; I don't really see how it would be much different, life would still suck, I'd still probably be angry, it's hard to see what harm he really has done to me. My friend *did* tell me though, that I seem different, obviously because of Ketten," Peter finished, with an ashamed look resting on his face.

There was a long pause.

The Judge thought it was his turn for input, "Tha—," he started, but was interrupted by Peter who jumped back into talking without any sort of acknowledgement that the Judge had begun to speak,

"And I realized all this because James told me I seemed different and that triggered all of these things, *I* couldn't even see it! *I* don't even know who *I* am; he has become such a part of me that I can't even tell the difference between what is him and what is me. I don't know who I'd be without him," he said somberly. "And," he said looking straight down at his feet, becoming overwhelmed by the remembrance of the visual to which he was subject about a week previous. Almost ashamed, he continued, "I saw something." He paused again. "Something that the words: 'sordid,' or '*vile*,' don't even suffice to aptly describe. And, if *that* is what Ketten has been leading me to, then I want nothing to do with him anymore," Peter declared firmly, sniffling.

When he eventually looked back up at the Judge, he had bloodshot eyes, saturated by the welled up tears. He was ready for change.

"This dog and his doings, are not congruent with the way you would ideally like to have your life be," the Judge felt impelled to share that with Peter.

Peter just sat shaking his head, his gaze not resting on any present object in the room.

It became quiet and still.

The Judge felt it necessary to let this moment teach Peter.

Peter was now faced with a grand choice: continue to exist under jurisdiction of the monster that had torn his life to shreds, or brush aside the shreds and start new from the shambles—bloom out of the wreckage. He was visibly lost, mentally. He was at a crossroads, and his eyes darted back and forth as if he were examining each path. He then looked to the Judge with a face of grief.

"Peter, you like music don't you?" asked the Judge.

Peter nodded.

"Do you know what a crescendo and a diminuendo are?"

"I think," replied Peter confidently, but unsure.

"A crescendo is the gradual increase of volume or intensity, and a diminuendo: the gradual *decrease*."

"Right, right." Peter nodded assertively.

"And, do you know what a bridge is?"

"The best part of the song!"

"Yes, very good. Now, Peter, let me illustrate: you are at a 'diminuendo' in your life right now. Now, with this desire, which you have, however big or small, we can take that and turn this diminuendo into a crescendo. And, with your willingness and my help, we can lead up to the bridge of your life. The bridge. Often the most powerful and most memorable segment of a song. We will make this part of your life the most powerful and memorable segment—thus far at least—resounding throughout the rest of your existence as something, on which you can reflect and from which you can gain strength when needed. An echoing powerful resistance and drastic conversion from chaos to peace. Peter, this will be tremendously difficult and arduous; you are at war, war has never been easy. But you *can* do it. I must also note that this 'bridge' *will* end; don't expect to have a never-ending crescendo after this is all said and done. You *will* still experience alternating diminuendos and crescendos, just like almost any piece of music. But, Peter, that is what makes a song beautiful, isn't it?" the Judge concluded, smiling.

Peter wept.

There was a small beam of light that glimmered in his heart; that light was hope.

~ CHAPTER 10 ~

THE CRESCENDO

It was a beautiful day. Peter could be found soaking it all in on the top of his favorite peak to climb. There he gained more insight, as well as in the process of climbing. For him, it was a perfect channel of understanding—it was his language, into which such a metaphorical profundity was translated for reception. He sat serenely, watching the birds flow through the sky like a windy river. With each deep breath, he took in new life and expelled the toxins that had been coursing through his system injected by Ketten's attachment. Taking in the beauty of the landscape pushed out the patterns of thinking and behavior, which Ketten had conditioned him to adopt—little by little. When Peter's cup was overflowing, he decided to head down, occasionally stopping to look up to get another glimpse at the view, that he could almost not bear to leave. He planned to walk straight to the Judge's house. As he descended the mountain, his level of fear ascended and started to crowd out the tranquility. He was leery and uncomfortable entering back into vulnerability.

He made his way swiftly to the Judge with steadfast focus. When he arrived, the Judge was surprised by his unease; Peter was shaky, paranoid and speaking fast.

"Everything alright, Peter?" asked the Judge with concern.

"Yeah. Yeah, yeah, no, no everything is all right now. It's all good, boss. All is well. No worries here," he said.

"Okay then," replied the Judge, giving a suspicious look, "go ahead and have a seat, I'll be right in."

Peter went to his self-designated chair. He let his nerves unwind a little bit.

When the Judge came back in he said, "Peter! Rest your shoulders, you look so tense!"

Peter was energized, and he didn't quite know exactly why. "Do I?" he asked, rubbing his knees, "Sorry, I just came down from the mountain, which was really great, but then I was afraid that I would run into Ketten. I feel like I've been more afraid of him lately. Luckily I haven't seen him around, otherwise I might rationalize like

I usually do and then get sucked in and lose myself with him."

The Judge showed his approval, "Very wise, Peter. I esteem your unwaveringness and unshaken efforts. Take heart, don't disregard the fact that you are aiming toward a worthy goal and doing your best to hold true to it."

Peter sort of brushed that off.

"So, why are you here exactly right now?" asked the Judge.

"Hey, it just occurred to me, why aren't you at the courthouse? Shouldn't you be working? You seem to have an awful lot of time," Peter flagrantly slid past the Judge's question and into his own,

The Judge laughed, "Well, couldn't I ask *you* the same thing?" he said smirking. "And may I say kindly that you occasionally tend to come off a tad careless and discourteous," said the Judge, sipping his drink.

Although his comment wasn't as accusatory as before, Peter admitted he was a bit forward, but was defensive and a bit offended, "Hey! I was going to get to answering your question, I just was curious about your work, and if I don't state what's on my mind right away, it disappears."

"Impatience," said the Judge with reproof raised his eyebrows, took another sip. The Judge was not angry or frustrated with Peter.

Peter, however, became more defensive in response and insulted, "Arrogance. And pretentiousness," with a look on his face of assumed glory for one-upping the Judge.

The Judge laid it to rest as he observed *Peter*'s frustration. "I have a trial in approximately 45 minutes, if you would like to join me, you may," invited the Judge.

Peter felt awkward now. He looked away and clenched his jaw tightly.

"So, *anyways*," Peter was clearly annoyed, "I just wanted to tell you about my mountain experience and my paranoia," he said sighing.

"Alright, what would you have me know, Peter?" asked the Judge attentively.

"Well," began Peter, still annoyed, but still desirous to share his thoughts and feelings, "I just felt this morning that it had been a long time since I've gone on a hike or climb, so I went for it, and I'm *so* glad I did. It was so calm and peaceful up there. Also, I realized something, well, actually a few things, but one thing is that Ketten never follows me up the mountain. Although regrettably, the amount of times I've fled to the mountain has been relatively few, which I think is a consequence or result of having that dumb dog around, because I love the mountains and climbing, so I wish I did it more. In any case, I've noticed that's one place he doesn't follow me, or show up. Well, actually, there was one time, we were like at the bottom of the mountain," he paused, remembering the moment with disdain, "that was the first time I saw him kill something: that little bird. He didn't follow me up the mountain. No, wait! I didn't even go up the mountain that time. I went and got ice cream. So, I don't know, I was just trying to make a correlation between when he does and doesn't show up," he thought out loud. As he talked more about the issue his annoyance was traded for concern and eagerness for counsel.

The Judge sensed this eagerness for counsel, knowing that he was obviously the young man's source of said counsel, he decided to withhold the counsel and test Peter instead. "And?" he said probingly.

"And what?" Peter screeched. "I told you all that so that *you* could tell me what it means! You don't even *know* what it means do you? This is just a cop-out on your part, isn't it?" he accused.

"Peter," the Judge started, but was suddenly interrupted.

"No! No, don't worry, you don't need to explain yourself, I'll just tell you what I'm supposed to make of it myself!"

The Judge raised his eyebrows with agreeing surprise.

"Well, basically the mountains are just my refuge and Ketten destroys everything I love," he said with pigheaded confidence, holding a face of assumed triumph over the Judge again.

The Judge nodded, impressed.

Peter's face was slowly won over by a look of awe that what he had spit out was actually quite sound. His stubbornness fled the scene, and he went with what he had discovered on his own. "Yeah! So I can break away to the mountains to escape Ketten, I'll just go there all the time! And then with the whole bird thing, that's just more evidence that I should ditch him; he literally just distorts my view of everything, twisting it so that everything beautiful becomes corrupt and foul," he cogitated, "Yeah," pausing more, "I don't like that," he said looking past the floor.

"Well done, Peter. I am impressed. Good analyses and self-awareness. However, may I suggest that you still remain aware; I address this because you said that you could just *escape* Ketten by going to the mountains; that is a commendable and feasible solution, but might I remind you that you said you were using Ketten as a 'substance.' A substance. A medication, implying only that you have a disease, an illness, an infection *within. Ketten* isn't the problem; he is the 'cure' that you have adopted, which is ironically obliterating you the more you believe it is actually curing you. And if you run away from Ketten, then you are subjecting yourself to the same conduct, by which Ketten was able to corrupt you—running away from your problems. You may, no, you *will* face other 'Kettens' in your life, and you will *always* have inner turmoil, neither of which you will ever have any sort of control over. You *must* have a coping mechanism in place, a way to find peace—real peace. You cannot escape them and if you try to it will just be like each time you run to Ketten now, and heeding the same results. Fixing the surface issue may help, but that would be simply avoidance, you have to change *you*. It will be painful, but necessary. Think of a crutch; at some point after a severe injury, you need to remove the crutch to put weight on the leg to allow proper healing. This process can be long, painful and uncomfortable, but you need to dispose of the crutch, you can't use it forever; you must become self-sustainable, self-reliant—and that doesn't mean selfish or stubborn. You can probably relate somewhat to this analogy, as I recall, you had a cast on your broken arm the first time I met you. I want you to meditate deeply on what this separation from Ketten will mean for you."

Peter was distracted a few times during the lengthy lecture, but for the most part he was honed in, intent on gathering as much information as he could to use to his benefit. He nodded throughout and at the end of the Judge's remarks.

"Peter, I hope I have made myself abundantly clear, and I apologize for the incoherent, unarticulated mess of words, I'm actually rather embarrassed, but there is simply too much that cannot be left unsaid on the matter. I know I am usually more concise, but I care for you, Peter, and I think I have a pretty good idea of what you can become, and these are things I have gathered from others' comparable ordeals." The Judge froze as if he was debating something in his mind. "And my own," he shared, with a relieved contentment on his face.

Peter sensed this was very personal and didn't inquire further out of respect, but took note. He was more touched by the fact that this meant the Judge perhaps trusted him, and also that he was a real person too. He felt slightly weird about the Judge caring for him, but thought it was nice. "Wow, thanks, Judge," he said with a smile, letting all his counsel trickle in.

"Well, would you like to head off to my trial with me? If not, I am comfortable leaving you here to hang around for the time being, if you would prefer."

Peter was intrigued by the offer, but declined, "Nah, I think I'm gonna stick with you."

"Alright, swell. I would be glad if you joined me."

And they headed off together to the courthouse.

When they arrived there were 4 cases that had to be taken care of. Peter was much more softhearted and open-minded than during his last visit, he sat anxious to see *these* cases pan out. Peter sat in the same seat as last time and was deeply engaged in the happenings. He observed everything, took everything in. The Judge came out to his desk, everyone stood up; this time Peter was trying to establish what may be the reasons for the Judge's unorthodox method, rather than trying to find reasons to victimize him. He sat down and listened. The first two persons were a man and then a woman. Their wrongdoings were very similar to those of all of the other accused. They were both "pardoned with a charge to keep the law," as most people are; the only thing that was really of any interest to note for Peter was that the woman was the first he'd seen. The third person was a surprise for Peter to see; it was the man that owned the small ice cream joint, which he frequented. He knew that man, and at least from their small exchanges (though on an irregular basis), Peter deemed the man pleasant, he conceived that this was a good man. When the man was beckoned to come before the Judge, Peter was certain he would be receive mercy. Because of this, his mind shut off, neglecting the reading off of the catalogue of crimes, awaiting the actual sentencing.

There was an extensive, thick silence before the Judge made a decision, or before he voiced it. It was as if the Judge was listening for something. He was searching deeply. The man seemed unaffected by the silence or suspense. Peter, on the other hand was dying. The Judge finally spoke up, "Isolated conversion. Length to be determined at a later period in time," he said calmly. Peter was shaken. He felt like his trust (though already somewhat feeble) wavered, for he obviously disagreed with the verdict. He could not comprehend why. His mind ran in circles for the remainder of the trial trying to understand, not paying any attention to the final ruling. He felt like he knew better than the Judge and was going to let him have it the second he saw him again.

As soon as the trial ended, Peter stood up to go and directly confront the Judge, but he quickly left the courtroom through a door close to his desk, not giving Peter any time to talk to him. He waited outside the courtroom for the Judge. As he was waiting, he heard a door opened and saw two men walking out, one of them the Judge,

"Hey!" Peter yelled to the Judge.

"Peter, I apologize, I have no time, I have some work to do. In the meantime you can go back to my house and wait for me there, I should be there within the hour or so," replied the Judge, turning hastily to continue about his work.

Peter sighed in frustration, and left to walk around outside shaking his head. He made tracks for the Judge's house, when suddenly he was stopped, "Are you freaking kidding me?" he muttered to himself. He found himself standing opposite his vice: Ketten. The dog sat there, ears perked up, tongue hanging out, staring down Peter. He was filled with adrenaline, a flush of intensity, with his heart beating three times faster than just a few moments ago. He knew how good it felt to let go and let Ketten take him away from everything, but he also knew how corrupt he becomes when this poisonous blight taps into his mind, although he didn't quite understand *how*; it was just a dog. He inched towards him; Peter became tenser. Ketten came up and nudged his nose against Peter's hand and leg, then began to bark. Peter, alarmed by the barking, didn't want to bring attention to him, as there was a plethora of people nearby that began to look. He tried to quiet the dog, but he wouldn't relent. Ketten then started to jump up and down and sprinted around the corner; for the split second he was gone, Peter was relieved that he got rid of him. Ketten then shattered his relief, swiftly returning to Peter, still barking, and motioning for him to come around the corner. Peter's curiosity was peaked. He badly wanted to see what he was trying to show him, and also wanted the barking to cease. He followed his gesturing around corner after corner, with growing frustration after each empty, unfulfilled corner turned. Ketten got him.

It wasn't until the next day that Peter saw the Judge. He showed up at his house around the same time as the previous day.

"Peter! What happened yesterday? You never came over," inquired the Judge, concerned but also slightly teasing him. Noticing that Peter must have had an unpleasant experience—due to his muteness—he invited him in so that they could discuss the events that had apparently taken place.

Peter sat, "He did it again, I can't believe it, I was doing so good too! That bas—,"

"Who?" the Judge interrupted,

"Who do you think?" That stupid dog! What does he want from me? I don't get it, he's just a dog, or, maybe he's not, I mean, he *must* not be, he's just a canker, a plague! He just gets in my mind, and seizes control. Or is it just me? Why in the blazes can't I figure this out?"

"Peter, let me remind you of the definition of a crescendo—it's *gradual*. I think that's really all that needs to be said," counseled the Judge.

Peter let that sink in.

"You're a good, capable young man, Peter, I trust you can do this, just let your desire, however deep inside or clouded, drive you to your destination; step out of the darkness and into the light," he said with assurance.

Peter felt the light of hope again, as well as anger, but this time it was a good anger.

"I can tell you're angry, Peter, that is good, so long as it remains directed at the behavior, motivating you to take the steps necessary to crush and vanquish this demon of your soul, and *never* at you or who you are, okay?" The Judge showed some emotion in that bit of advice.

"Peter, this wretched creature nor the hell, in which it has created for you to reside does not define you," the Judge said with such a firmness that Peter knew the Judge was undeniably sincere; his gaze was riveted on Peter.

Peter is not the best at keeping eye contact. "I appreciate that, Judge. I just feel, like, possessed when he shows up, I don't know what it is, but I don't like it…all I want is just to find a wife, and just have little mini-me's runnin' around, be real good at guitar, and climb mountains all the time, and ya know I guess Ketten is just standing in the way of that dream, so screw him, I'm done, I'm out!" he added defiantly.

"Then go get it, Peter, there isn't anything or anyone stopping you," said the Judge smiling.

"Yeah, except for a rabid demon beast some people call a dog!" Peter quipped. He felt reenergized and refreshed upon leaving the Judge's house.

The Judge was happy to see him with this revived motivation.

On his way home, Peter was looking up. He didn't even feel fear of Ketten, except for one instance when he caught a glimpse of a dog in his peripheral, but was calmed when he saw it was a different dog entirely, with a white coat.

~ CHAPTER 11 ~

THE BRIDGE

Peter, again on the mountaintop, randomly felt woozy, and decided it was time to head back. He realized that he had not inquired about the meaning of the asinine decision for the convicted ice cream man. He had to replay the trial in his head. He gathered the slue of questions that penetrated his mind from the meditation. Additionally, during the descent, this wooziness led him to drift off into a daydream. He started to hear a certain song play out loud: one of his favorites, and he bobbed his head back and forth to the beat. Then, several boulders started crashing down the mountainside around him, followed by a herd of mountain goats, which pranced down the mountain. Peter, unfazed by the bizarre sights, continued down the trail, not questioning, but rather imagining he was part of some sort of music video, singing along with the lyrics. Peter was only stopped in his tracks when he caught a glimpse in the corner of his eye, of what looked like himself, chasing a rogue goat. After a few seconds, the

goat-chasing Peter turned to the deer-in-headlights Peter
and said, "Why are you so afraid?" Peter's mind shot
straight to Andy, when he asked him the very same
question before he died, "Step out of the darkness and into
the light," he then said. Peter recalled the Judge saying this
verbatim. Lastly, Peter was asked, "What are you doing?"
by the fabricated Peter, sending him into a spiraling
introspection. Suddenly, the Judge walked up to goat-
chasing Peter from behind (which from a distance looked
as if he rose out of the ground, like the sun), and placed his
arm on his shoulder, "He's right, Peter," he said. "Peter.
Peter!" Peter, hearing his name shouted, turned to see
where it was coming from and found Ketten yelling at
him. He blinked and snapped out of it, realizing he was in
the middle of the Town square, with an angry mother
yelling at her child, coincidentally named Peter.

Now Peter had something to think about during
his travel to the Judge's. Peter, in a daze, opened the door
and welcomed himself into the Judge's house, walking
straight to his chair, looking down all the while as if trying
to read the meaning like it was placed in an owner's
manual in front of him.

After several minutes, the Judge entered the room;
"Alright then," he said not expecting to find a confused

Peter inside his house without his knowledge, "Peter, I could have been naked. What would you have done then?" said the Judge, not angrily, but rather informatively.

Peter looked at him with a blank face, unentertained.

"Just a thought," he added.

Peter was still unresponsive and inattentive.

"I mean it's just a *nice* thing to do; courtesy, common sense," the Judge prodded for any response, receiving none. "So what's on your mind?" he finally asked.

"Welp, two things: I still wanted to talk about the trial from the other day, and I just had the oddest daydream." He thought for a second, which he'd rather address first, and because he wanted to save the most protuberant or in-depth topic for last, he chose to tell about the daydream first. He explained it very sporadically—so much so that the Judge responded in laughter. Peter was irritated by that, "C'mon! I'm serious, can you tell me what it means?" he said, with a tone of impatience.

"Peter, I am no fortuneteller or 'dream interpreter,'" said the Judge chuckling, "do you feel that it has a specific meaning, that it's trying to speak to you in some way?"

"Well, yeah! But I just don't know *what*! I mean *I* show up, in my own dream, and quote Andy, and you. Ketten and you also both show up, *that* alone has got to mean something significant, and what they said too." He tried to put all the pieces together.

"Yes, Peter, you've got it!" said the Judge, seemingly nonchalantly, but in actuality, once again, allowing Peter to figure it out on his own.

Peter, now preoccupied with this annoyance that the Judge didn't care (according to his perception), was unable to come to a conclusion.

The Judge reassured Peter, "You'll get it, don't worry. Right now, I must get ready for another trial, do you wish to accompany me again or stay here and think?"

"I guess I'll come," replied Peter stubbornly.

They got their things together and made their way to the courthouse.

As Peter sat through this trial, his thoughts were mostly absent from the goings-on in the courtroom. He sat slouched in his seat, lethargic and aloof. Then suddenly, he was greeted by a random thought; he wondered what he would do if he were caught and brought before the Judge. He countered with a self-righteous attitude, that he's not doing anything wrong, he's the *victim*. He entered into a conversation with himself, puffing himself up, saying that there's nothing wrong with "Peter," dodging any sort of self-guilt, eluding all blame, laying that aside on Ketten and anyone else he could think of. Like a slap in the face, he was revisited by his goat-chasing self, reprimanding him, asking, "What are you doing?" as in the daydream. It hit him, "What *am* I doing?" he asked himself. He stepped out of the self-praising, and into self-evaluation. "I haven't done freaking *anything* with my life!" he thought to himself; he dwelt on this for a while letting it fall into place, revolving around that idea that he didn't even know what he was doing or where he was going. He remembered a song lyric that in essence described how humans rarely know themselves because they're too concerned about other people's lives. He concluded he didn't really know himself too well. He also became partially excited to share his newfound awareness.

Peter and the Judge arrived back at the mansion after the trial. Peter saved the most monumental discussion for when they were in a sit-down environment. Once the atmosphere was set, according to how Peter would ideally have it be (without any distractions or upcoming diversions), he began to convey that, which he'd learned while he mentally checked out of the trial and dissected the daydream. "I basically just discovered that I don't even know who I am, what I'm doing or where I'm going. I have lost *myself*. My 'mirror image' was right. I guess I've just gotten to the point where I'm stagnant and waiting for something better to simply fall into my lap, but *I'm* not really doing anything to move in any useful direction. I also realized how much I was blaming everything or everyone especially Ketten of course," Peter taught himself as the monologue continued. "I mean how could I not though? *He's* done all of this! It's like I keep seeing a shiny gold coin glimmering in a pile of dirt and when I dig to pick it up, it disappears, and then when I go to leave, it glimmers again, luring me in, so I keep digging to find it and pretty soon before I know it I've dug myself into a giant pit that I can't climb out of, *and* when I finally get the gold coin it ends up being counterfeit! But I guess *I'm* still the one doing the digging," Peter became disheartened. "I just feel so dilapidated and decrepit. I put myself here and I am failing at life. I've wasted so much time."

The Judge stepped in, "Peter, you're *not* a waste of space. And you're *only* a failure if you stop trying. If you were running a marathon and tripped and fell flat on your face during the first mile, would you just give up and quit?

Discouragement comes, and doubt comes but you embrace them, and then let it go. Just quit worrying, and don't give up. Good times are ahead," consoled the Judge.

Peter nodded in reluctant agreement, "Ya know, I really hate those sappy, 'inspirational,' messages, like 'you can do it,' and all that cheesy, corny stuff, but I really needed to hear that. Thanks Judge!" said Peter, looking up.

"Let me explain something to you, Peter, there is a great deal of liars in this world. Many spiders claiming to be butterflies, snakes claiming to be sparrows, wolves to be sheep, and so on. It is all simply a façade, and underneath lies the ugly truth, a venomous viciousness, awaiting the total destruction of either themselves or others. No matter how 'tough' any one person portrays him or herself to be, we all need aid. Everyone crumbles and needs to be picked up. There is a personal individualized hell, a storm, for all. But you know what, Peter? Storms pass, pits can be climbed out of. Life is violent and callous, but humans *can* survive, you *can* conquer. We can all muster up the strength, we may have to dig it up and dust it off, but it is there inside all of us. No one is exempt from armistice, liberation and rest, but it *is* conditional, and comes in fragments. And life *can* be marvelous!" the Judge illuminated with fervor, "Do you understand, Peter?"

"Yeah, I do: acceptance," he confirmed.

The Judge nodded.

Peter felt light. He asked politely for a cup of water, and when the Judge went to fetch it, Peter stood up and walked to the window to breathe deeply. He folded his arms and took in the view of the whole Town, and the mountainside being enveloped in dark, dense clouds. Peter personally loved the rain, and wasn't emotionally affected by it, as many are. He chuckled at the coincidentally apt timing for this storm to approach as they had just spoken of the passing of certain stormy threats. He faced the storm squarely, envisioning it as a storm of life, and felt ready to take it on.

The Judge reentered the room with the glass of water and some crackers.

"Oh joy! Thanks Judge you're just simply the best! Just a true saint," said Peter playfully. He returned to his seat, "So, tell me about the method to your madness," he said very eagerly.

"I'll assume you are referring to my method of sentencing people," said the Judge almost patronizingly, "W—,"

The Judge was immediately interrupted by Peter, "Yeah! Is it all just at random? How do you decide who to put away and who to let go? Does it even work? Where do all the people end up? Why did you lock up the ice cream man?" Peter fired off questions like a Gatling gun.

The Judge paused, checking if he had finished, and then asked, "Peter, have you ever met any of the people, whom I have pardoned?"

Peter was about to answer in the affirmative, but caught himself and thought about it for a second, "Hmm, no I guess I haven't. Is there a reason for that? Why do you ask?" he asked skeptically.

"Peter, you're being ridiculous. Keep an eye out for them, it's a small Town, I'm sure you'll run into one eventually. Talk to the people that you meet throughout the day, in some way, whether great or small, I have dealt with almost all of them. You can see for yourself what *they* think, what it does for *them*. All I would say on the matter is that I know what I am doing, Peter. It's not just some social experiment. There is *extreme* difficulty in finalizing these decisions. It is *never* easy to dictate what these people need. That's why the timing is so crucial; the Witnesses work hard and do a tremendous job of bringing people in when they are ready."

"So, I noticed you said '*dictate,*'" said Peter, implying a further clarification.

"It is all based on where their heart is," unsure of how Peter would translate that, the Judge refined it, "that is to say, where they've been and where they are going. Peter, I don't make any decisions based on a 'hunch,' nor are they based on any preconceived notions I may have towards the person. When they are brought before me, it is generally in the best possible state for being *molded*," The Judge answered confidently.

Peter thought in his mind that this only raises more questions, for example, how the Judge "knows people's hearts," and what he means by "molding."

The Judge added one final bit of information: "My purposes always remain the same—I wish to bring greater harmony to these people, to this Town. This takes both time, and individualized focus, for everyone is different, and walks at a different pace. People have simply become ignorant to, or warped, disfigured, and fractured their views on these, my purposes. Whether *they* see it or not, what I do is vital."

Peter pondered. He could not think of any further counterarguments or interrogative inquiries.

Several months have passed. Peter walks through the center of Town on his way to the Judge's home. He has been visiting with the Judge on a regular basis. He has still observed much of the vandalism and thievery and violence that takes place, at times more personally than others. There have been a few encounters with Ketten, but at only one of which, he slipped, handing himself over to the grip of Ketten, seeking to fill the void. He since picked himself up and flushed out the aftertaste of Ketten's foul fruit. He is seeing that each fall provides another rung to the ladder by which he can ironically climb out of the very pit into which he falls.

As Peter is walking, harmonious melodies fill his head; he is lifted by the mentally broadcasted concert. As he hums the harmony to the song, he recalls the Judge's labor for harmony, and he sees this in his own life now. He smiles. At this moment, he knows that everything is *good*. He looks at the clouds, at the shops, at the people passing by. He sees a mother with a small child trying to eat ice cream, but instead wearing it on his face and hand; two kids race by on their bikes joyously; a father carrying his daughter on his shoulders; birds flying overhead; a cool-looking white dog; a taco stand. He is sold; he'll buy a taco before he goes to see the Judge. The taco just makes him that much happier.

He arrives at the Judge's, "Hey, Judge! How you been? It's been a minute now hasn't it?" he asked enthusiastically, walking in the door.

"I'm doing well, Peter, how have *you* been doing?" asked the Judge in return, equally enthused.

"Well, I just ate a taco, so I'm doing fantastic!"

"Terrific! I am genuinely glad to hear that, Peter," said the Judge with a huge smile, as they sat in their designated seating arrangement.

"Yeah, ya know life is good, it used to be lackluster at best, but now, I mean I eat tacos all the time, I go climbing a lot, been also jammin' on my new guitar tons; there's just not much to complain about right now. It's just a 'no-worries' kinda life, you know what I'm talking about, Judge, I'm basically a hippie!"

"That is good. Keep it that way! I also wanted to ask, how was your birthday, Peter?"

"It was really great, I feel officially old, but I bought the guitar with money I got for my birthday, and it sounds so good!"

The Judge laughed, "Twenty-four is not 'old,' Peter!"

Peter laughed and shrugged his shoulders.

He was excited to share every bit of news that he had; "But, yeah, I just feel so *cleansed*, like my chakras are all clearing out and opening up!"

The Judge chuckled, "'Chakras,' eh? Someone's been studying Hinduism."

Peter winked and continued speaking, "Stoked on life. Oh! Did I tell you I've taken up pottery? I'm really gettin' into it! I started a couple weeks back; plus, it's got its perks," he said with a devilishly giddy smirk. "And this 'perk' happens to be named Berlin. And her unique and interesting name makes her even more gorgeous!"

The Judge was elated, "Ah yes! You mentioned her briefly the last time we spoke, how are things with this female?"

"Things are going *swimmingly* as they say! Like I said, we met at my pottery class, and so I see her at least every time I have class, and we've been on a few dates as well. She is just, remarkable!" he chuckled at himself, "Remarkable? I mean she is, but it sounds like I'm turning into *you* with words like that!" Peter was giddy. "Yeah, she just makes me feel so great! I'm just so happy! I've really ever only *dreamed* about this feeling; I would catch glimpses of it every time I looked out on the birds when I was on the mountain."

"Yes, Peter, this is indeed the apex of your life. The bridge—chorally, tonally, symphonically, if you will, the most beautifully momentous in comparison with all other times in your life thus far. Don't allow it to pass by you without being enjoyed. There is already, visibly much greatness surrounding you, and I believe even that a great deal of greatness is yet to come; it is not seen right now, however, it *will* come based on the way you are choosing to live your life at this stage of it," professed the Judge.

"How wonderful! Visible and invisible greatness. Isn't that great?" Peter said laughing humbly.

~ CHAPTER 12 ~

PEACE

Peter, since discussing the Judge's processes of bringing harmony to the Town, has coincidentally come in contact with a few of the Judge's aforementioned pardoned and incarcerated, as the Judge had suggested Peter do. These coincidences are similar to the effect of when someone mentions a certain song that you've never heard, and suddenly you begin to hear it almost everywhere you go, as Peter describes it. The first one that Peter stumbled upon was found in the convenience store, when Peter was buying chocolate milk and potato chips. He overheard a couple talking in the aisle over about the Judge, his ears perked up. Peter was determined to learn how the Judge was perceived among the people and what sort of influence the Judge's practice was having on the Townspeople. Only good things were said, not much (anymore) to Peter's surprise.

Peter approached them; he actually did it with such vigor that the two people were worried for their own safety.

"How do you know the Judge?" he asked them directly.

Taken aback by his impolite intrusion and intensity, they hesitated to answer, "Uh, he helped us out once…and who are you again?" the man said.

"He did?" Peter said enthusiastically, smiling, "how did he help you out?" he investigated. Waiting for an answer that didn't come, he caught himself, "Oh, my name's Peter," he said, thinking that would suffice and waiting intently for the reply.

They saw his strange passion for the subject and figured he meant well, so they opened up, "About seven years ago, our oldest son was unexpectedly attacked and killed by some thug from the deep, dark part of Town. We struggled to pick ourselves up after that. We went to the trail to see cruel justice delivered to the brutish, pitiful excuse of a man, but we didn't see that happen. We added another person to our hate list: the Judge. We were sickened that we could share the same species with such monsters. After confronting the Judge, we simply couldn't believe how one could stoop to such a low level of ignorance. We started shifting our blame to the most prevalent face, forgetting about the killer. But, after many visits, we slowly started to see the deterioration of our resentment, a lifting of our pain, and an understanding and empathy that filled its place, reluctantly and begrudgingly at first of course, but indefinitely. He helped us see that this man, was just that: a *man*. This wasn't to *excuse* him, but rather a correlation, a connection. I don't know about you," said the woman to her husband, "but I *hated* that fact! How could *I* be in the same boat as *him*? But, you know it takes time, and we're at peace with it now," the mother said contently.

"Wow, that's fascinating. I appreciate you sharing that, it's been really helpful!" expressed Peter.

The couple, still a little confused, asked, "So, what was this for?"

Peter, oblivious to the fact that he had somehow left that bit of (very pertinent) information out, replied, "Oh, yeah so I'm working together with the Judge now, he is a remarkable man," Peter smiled at his word choice, "he has helped me a lot too, and I am just curious how he has helped the Town as a whole, and what part he has played in the current state of the Town. Do you guys know of anyone, who thinks negatively of him? Or of anyone who has been locked up?"

"Hmm, we don't know anyone personally who dislikes him, but I'm sure, sadly, that there are many. We have some friends who know someone who was locked up quite a few years ago, but we don't know anything about him now. Sorry, we're not much help," said the husband.

"Alright, that's okay, I'm sure I'll find some. Well it was nice to meet you and thank you again for the personal story."

They shook hands and said goodbye.

"Tell the Judge Dan and Julia said hello!" they requested.

"Okay! Will do," Peter replied, giving a thumbs up.

Peter started to make a mental list to keep track of all the encounters, as, now that he had found people on one end of the spectrum, he was more curious to find out how the Judge was construed by people of the other end. Over the course of the next 2 weeks, he became so enveloped by this task, that he didn't even go to see the Judge. He would walk about the Town, putting himself in the midst of all foot traffic and more densely populated parts of the Town at different times of the day to have a better chance of running into these differently-tried citizens, and he would listen with keener ears. Sometimes he would act like he was talking on the phone, and mention the Judge in his conversation while around people, just to see whose interest was peaked when his name was mentioned.

The next person he came across was a very meek middle-aged man. He came over to Peter after hearing his fake phone conversation, "Excuse me, pardon my rudeness, but I couldn't help but overhear you talking about your obligation to attend a trial with the Judge."

Peter smiled because his trick worked; the man had taken the bait. "Yes! So, you know the Judge?"

"I do indeed, my friend; the man changed my life," he declared proudly.

"Could you please tell me *your* story?"

The man simply supposed that Peter was just nervous to meet the Judge and wanted to alleviate his mind, "Oh, I'd be glad to. Well, I estimate it all started back when I was just a kid, probably no more than 7 or 8 years old. I was young, stupid, and reckless. Anything that I was told was 'the right thing to do,' I intentionally did the opposite. Well, I continued to get myself deeper into trouble, but somehow all the while avoiding any punishment. When I was about seventeen, I committed my first murder. Then, I *knew* that I would for certain be caught and punished severely, so I fled the Town. I up and left, and tried to find a new town on foot. Well, I guess I'm not that great at navigating because I think I passed out somewhere along the way after my exit, and when I awoke, I was back in the Town again! Don't know how…but, amidst all of this, I just tried to lay low and stay away from any more problems.

"I didn't do anything *really* bad like I had done before, for about a year, mainly out of fear. But then, I slowly started getting back into these bad behaviors and actions, and I found myself deeper and further than I had ever been before. I had done pretty much every evil thing imaginable. And, ironically, I believe the fear kept me there; that and desperation. Well, then, as expected, one day I was caught and taken before the Judge, and by that I mean, that in a drunken stupor, when I was oblivious and without strength or energy, they came and got me and I awoke in a holding cell (so I wouldn't escape) until the trial commenced. I was sentenced to one year of 'isolated conversion.'"

When the man said he had been "locked up," Peter realized he had hit the jackpot!

"I was just so depressed and out of it, I didn't really pay much mind or have any sort of response, I just didn't care, or wasn't awake enough, I don't really know, I guess perhaps I had just given up.

Anyways, I went to the cell, or room however you want to call it—which, by the way was actually quite nice living quarters, and the care, food, bed and all that, was very nice, I just never saw anyone. I went through many phases throughout the 12 months (and it *is* always 12 months—no compression, no extension, no getting out early on good behavior, not sure why, but that's the way it is). I was in that lifeless funk, derelict and limp. I was *dead*...lost. That lasted for a good portion of my stay there. Then a seed of hatred and blame was planted in me, aimed at the Judge, anger sprouted out of it, I was hell-bent on extracting all of my revenge. That lasted maybe a month, and then I switched over to hatred towards myself, that evolved into hatred of everyone and everything.

"Then, one day, it hit me; I became overwhelmed and sunk deep into awareness of all the things that I had done. Diseased by the guilt, the monstrous guilt. The lies. The torture I had put myself through and probably so many others. I was *crushed*. The remainder of my stay— which was no longer isolated...it felt like that guilt was a tangible personage, constantly present—was infested by these aching thoughts. I had to change. So, I did. And when I got out, I met with the Judge and thanked him for placing me there, and I continued to meet with him, for a number of months. He opened my eyes, he is a very genuine man; once *I* saw clearly, I discovered that this man, whom I had deemed my enemy, was actually not *evil* at all, no, he is just the opposite! I thank him that my life is now calm, it's still a constant 'marathon,' with its challenges, and ups and downs, but also its immense beauty and refreshment," the man finished contently, taking a deep breath.

"Wow, I can't believe I met someone who has been locked up, and I really appreciate you sharing your story with me, I know it's probably pretty personal. I am especially glad to hear your positive opinion of the Judge. It's nice to see his work not go unnoticed," said Peter. He noticed that he himself was beginning to value the Judge more as he heard people's validations of his service.

"Well, I think the term 'locked up' gives a sort of negative connotation, don't you think? And it is my pleasure. It *is* personal, but I don't mind sharing it, *because* it means so much to me. I also hope that your trial with the Judge goes well, don't worry about it, he is a very warmhearted man. My name is Raymond by the way."

Peter isn't confrontation's biggest fan, so he awkwardly ignored the comment about him going to a trial, "Nice to meet ya, Ray! I'm Peter. Hey, you have a great day, alright?"

"Well, I appreciate that, thanks Peter," said Raymond, smiling modestly.

Before Peter left, he remembered at the last second to ask one more thing, "Oh! Wait! Ray, do you know anyone else who was pardoned or loc—," he changed his wording, "I mean, isolated?" he threw out a word of which he was still unsure, "I'd really like to see their side."

"Uh, let's see. I only know a few people that I *used* to associate with that received the same sentence, however, I have no knowledge of their current whereabouts, or what has happened to them, but I know they were pretty rough fellows, so I wouldn't be surprised if they were right back where they started."

"Okay, thanks anyways!" Peter said satisfied.

Peter walked away feeling pretty lucky about all of these chance encounters, excited to find the next. While he was walking away, he glanced over towards the mountain and decided it was time for a hike. He quickly ran home got some supplies and headed straight for the mountain. While he was hiking, he had a strange thought pop in for a visit. He had a sudden strange urge, or desire to have a dog by his side. One of the reasons he started to have Ketten around was because he loved dogs. He was a bit disinclined to this idea, however, for obvious reasons, yet intrigued. He thought for a moment, and agreed that he still loved dogs, based on the fact that every time he saw one on the Town square, he became giddy and wanted to pet it. He consoled himself by the persuasive argument that Ketten was no ordinary *dog*, but rather an otherworldly creature disguised as a dog bent on destroying the boy Peter. "Yep, that's it," he said out loud to himself, then continued climbing.

As nightfall conquered the Town, Peter descended from the stone throne, and was injected into the bloodstream of the veins of the Town, flowing through alleyways and streets towards home. As he was walking, he heard footsteps behind him; his ears perked up, and he slowed his pace, alert, but remaining calm, and continuing forward not letting the shadowed presence know of his detection. The footsteps suddenly quickened and grew louder; Peter knew he was about to be ambushed. He prepared himself, and at just the right moment when the attacker was almost upon him, he swiftly ducked down, sending the attacker flying over him; the man was trying to tackle Peter, but it failed. Peter hurried and jumped on top of the man to hold him down, he spat in Peter's face.

"You dirtbag!" Peter yelled at the man, trying to wipe it off on his shoulder.

The man shouted, "Get off me, you little sh—,"

"Hey!" Peter barked, interjecting to shut him up, asserting his dominance in the situation. "Now, listen!" Peter started, and then stopped. He looked intently at the man.

The now uncomfortable man cried, "What? Whaddya want? What are you doing?" with a fear in his eyes.

Peter asked, "Don't I know you? Where do I know you from? Wait! You met with the Judge, didn't you? I saw you at a trial, yeah, that's it. Well, great! You were pardoned weren't you?" Peter inquired with an enthusiasm that was received by the man as very strange.

"The Judge? That numbskull?" retorted the man, with a demented laugh, "He's an idiot, don't know what in the name of the devil he is still doing as the judge. He is the stupidest man I know!"

Peter listened, intrigued to see the other side.

"He has no idea what he's doing, you know he has ulterior motives, don't ya? I'm certain he's getting paid the big bucks under the table somewhere, somehow just to screw this place up; it's a distraction! Something big is going to happen, it's a conspiracy! That's why it's everyone for themselves out here! No mercy! No one can be trusted! *Everyone* is evil! Ya know I'm surprised no one has gone and taken him out yet. Yeah. Maybe *I'll* rally up a mob, get some people together and go burn his house to the ground with him inside!" said the man with a wicked smirk and crazed look, chuckling.

"Shut up," responded Peter, releasing his hold on the man and standing up to leave.

"Oh, what? Did I offend you?" retorted the man on the ground, "You like the Judge? Well you're stupid too then, you're a *coward*!" he yelled and laughed.

Peter looked at him, scoffed, turned and walked away, shaking his head. The next day Peter couldn't help but notice that a small seed of doubt had been planted in his mind from the exchange with the deranged man on the ground.

About a week later, Peter went to visit the Judge. It had been a while (in which time he had also run into 3 other citizens who had all been pardoned, turned themselves around, and were respectably honest and moral people, according to what he observed), and he felt he needed the boost. He decided that it was time after he'd woken up from another strange dream—regarding Ketten. In short, in the dream he encountered a deer in a dark setting, and it appeared to be feeding on something. As he got closer, the deer was devouring the corpse of another animal. When he got even closer the deer quickly swung its head, displaying its bloodied antlers and face. Peter blinked and the deer had instantly transformed into Ketten, then he heard a demonic voice speak out as if it were from Ketten, saying, "Look on me and be afraid!" Peter was heavily perturbed by this.

He showed up at the Judge's and was welcomed just as warmly as each previous time. He walked to his chair, head drooping down.

The Judge noticed his gloom, and explored the cause thereof, "Peter, what's bothering you?"

Still looking down, Peter answered directly, "Berlin broke up with me."

The Judge nodded, grasping the full scope of his situation, "Aha, and how are you holding up?" aware that he was asking a question with a fairly obvious answer, the Judge dug to provoke a deeper sharing.

"Man, I just thought she was perfect, I thought *life* was perfect! Everything was going so well, I was imagining what our kids would look like with this girl! And now she breaks up with me and a couple other stupid things and I just feel like a pile of crap! I'm angry. I'm depressed. I'm lethargic and tired all the time. I'm just pissed and I hate everything," he said, laughing at how ridiculous he thought all of this was.

"Ok, what was her reasoning for ending the relationship?"

"I don't really know, I guess she just lost interest or something," said Peter with a lack of self-assurance.

"And could you please explain to me what the problem is?"

Peter looked at the Judge as if he had just insulted his mother, "I just *did*! My girlfriend just broke up with me! I guess she doesn't like Peter," he expressed, flustered.

"I understood that part, but I still have yet to see the problem, Peter," explained the Judge calmly, with a smile.

Peter rolled his eyes.

"Would you like me to spell it out for you, Peter?" the Judge smirked, "Is there anything wrong with one particular person not liking another particular person? Why are you so hung up on and offended by the fact that one girl lost interest in you? Suppose she decided to settle, despite the lack of interest, how do you imagine the relationship would have progressed? The point I'm trying to make is you may love watermelon and detest squash, but there is most *definitely* a person out there who is exactly the opposite, don't let that cause you to build barriers. Having distinctions among people is part of cohabitating the earth with a diverse population. People seem to take offense at such insignificant, petty and frankly *pathetic* dissimilarities between others these days."

Peter excused himself to use the bathroom. He let his mind grab hold of these thoughts and tried to decipher them, and see how they settled with him. When he finished washing his hands he stood staring at his reflection in the mirror with a look of contemplation. He felt an annoying feeling in the background of his cluttered emotions that the Judge was right, and he tried to accept these facts and forget about them temporarily. When he returned, the Judge asked him, "Did you fall in?" he chuckled.

Peter gave a weak laugh, and sat down.

The Judge knew he was contemplating and contending with his inner, deeper conscience. "What happened to your arm?"

"Huh?" Peter answered searching his arms, "Oh, this?" he pointed to a gash on his arm.

The Judge nodded.

"That's nothing, I just slipped a little when I was climbing the other day and scraped it pretty bad."

"Hmm, well it doesn't seem to be healing very well, are you picking at the scab?"

"Yeah, I heard that if you pick at the scab, the scar becomes more prominent, and I like scars, scars are cool," said Peter grinning.

"You know, Peter, you think that these physical scars are 'cool' and you flaunt them, but you are still so unnecessarily fretful about and burdened by the scars that others *cannot* see. I speak of the scars of your being. I perceive that you feel that you are scarred, tattered, and broken and simply *existing*, but Peter, you are an *exceptional* young man! You should be *living*!" The Judge choked up, "These things do not define you. It does not matter what other people think; what defines you lies beneath, on the *inside*." The Judge paused, seeking a response from Peter who was staring at the floor. He had unexpectedly struck a profound chord. The Judge saw a tear fall from his face to the ground.

"No, Judge, you're wrong." Peter opened up, "I've never told you, or *anyone* this, but did you know after Andy was killed, I went out…" He hesitated, "And I stole a knife from a pawn shop, and I, *hunted* for the man or the thugs that took Andy's life; I was intent on murdering them. I would have done it, had I found them, or really anyone that got in my way, I would have done it. It was weird because almost no one was out that night. I must have been out there for hours…all night. So, you see, Judge? I've been in dark places; I've been a *dark person*. I know things have been going well lately, well, except for *this*, but I still feel like I have darkness *in* me," Peter confessed.

The Judge sighed, "Peter, did you not listen to anything that I just said?"

"Uhh, did *you* listen to a word *I* said? You're over here giving your lengthy anecdotes and I'm over here pouring my heart out!" he said firmly.

"And I'm telling you that none of that *matters*, Peter. It is in your *past*; therefore it is *behind* you. Why do you keep turning around? Who cares about your past, all that matters is who you are now; who you are now is a reflection of how you handled your past. And who you *are* is a remarkable person! Don't be deceived!" proclaimed the Judge, once again becoming passionate.

Peter was taking the truth to be hard, still reluctant to fully embrace it, the wrestle was visible on his face, "But," he attempted to interject and counter the Judge, but was denied.

"Peter, remember; the apex was a singular point, not a plateau, just as the past does not determine what kind of person you are, neither does the rocky terrain ahead. Do not ever let yourself envision a perfect life, or even wife for that matter, because you will almost certainly *always* be let down, life will be hard, relationships and other things take time, just keep going, *let go*, move on."

Peter sighed and closed his eyes; he submitted, and embraced it. He knew that this was going to take a little bit of time to settle in, however. He told the Judge that he was going to need to come back another time, as he still needed to give him his report about his observations of the Town. They bid farewell, and upon leaving, Peter, not too far from the Judge's house, encountered the white dog he had seen previously just sitting on the corner of the sidewalk, looking up at him, who gave a confused look in return.

The Judge wasn't too worried about his hasty exit; he knew he just needed time to let these things soak in.

A few days later, a recharged and renewed Peter came to the Judge's house, who wasn't present at the time. He assumed that he was at a trial, and decided to bum around nearby until he returned. He headed up behind his house, which was right on the mountainside. He was delighted to see a labyrinth of different trails drizzled across the face of the mountain. As he was hiking around, he enjoyed the trees, the view, the wildlife—including the birds, and also stumbled upon the mysterious white-colored canine. He stood staring at it confused again. He searched his feelings and attempted to determine what sort of connection this might suggest. The dog seemed so calm. He thought back to his strange desire to have a four-legged companion again. In his reservoir of feelings, he could not find any suspicion, despite the fact that he is typically suspicious and untrusting, not to mention anything regarding Ketten. Neither could he even find any curiosity; he just felt content. He concluded that that was evidence enough that *this* dog would not lead him to anything like to what Ketten did. He walked around with him for a little bit until he caught a glimpse of the Judge returning home, at the sight of which he scurried down the mountain to greet him.

The Judge giggled when he saw Peter scampering down the slope, "Is that a wild gazelle I've spotted?" he called out jestingly.

Peter met the Judge cheerfully, "Salutations, sir Judge," he smirked, and they went inside.

The Judge started to head for the kitchen.

Peter stopped him, "Hold up, Judge, where you goin'? There's no need for crackers, I've got cookies right here!" he said, pulling a sleeve of cookies out of his pocket with an enormous grin. He felt good about his small gesture.

The Judge was delighted too. "Well, *thank you*, Peter, that was very thoughtful."

They sat down and got situated.

The Judge brought out the glasses of water. "So what were you doing up on the mountain while I was gone?" asked the Judge.

"Oh, nothing really, just killing time, I showed up and you weren't here, so I went exploring," Peter smiled. He skipped over the part about the white dog, not sure how he himself felt about it yet, therefore not sure how much of a benefit it would be to publicize the occurrence in the company of the Judge. He also felt no need to discuss the topic of the previous visit, as he has mulled it over and come to terms that the Judge was right.

"So, I met a lot of people that know you," Peter said vaguely, wanting to report his findings.

"Oh, is that so?" replied the Judge, grinning at Peter's unconventional methods of conversing.

"Yeah. There's lots of people that hate you," he said frankly.

The Judge nodded with an intrigued look on his face.

"I met people who are themselves and who know others who are at pretty much all ends of the spectrum. I saw…a gap. It's strange, I've never really noticed this before, but you can see, or maybe *feel* is the better word for it, a difference. Like night and day just within the Town. There are certain parts of the Town that harbor just more darkness, blackness, and then other parts that are just lighter, there's just a brighter, aura?" He said searching for the right words to give an apt enough description. "No wonder I felt so bad inside, and got caught up with Ketten, I was always wandering around in those parts of Town," he learned.

The Judge was impressed, "Wow, Peter I must say, I am surprised that you were able to detect that. You observed firsthand the nature of this Town," the Judge commended.

Peter accepted his praise and continued, "But it seemed like there were so many good people, it seemed like they outnumbered the bad, so why isn't the Town a better place then?" he asked pondering.

"I ask myself the same question nearly every day, Peter. But, I am not in control of making people's decisions for them. Sadly, the people get deceived. Some are lured in by the tantalizing and seemingly rewarding lifestyle that the darkness has to offer. Changing one from one side to the other, particularly from darkness light is long and arduous—gradual, as you know—but you just have to show them a little mercy and compassion," the Judge explained, using terms that Peter is capable of straightforwardly understanding.

This made sense to Peter, so he didn't trifle with it, "There's still just one thing I can't seem to figure out. I know *that* you have helped these people, or done all you can, most of them return the favor and are dedicated to this better life you have given them so to speak, others not so much, they are blinded and misguided. I understand *what* you are doing, your work and the aim, and *how* you are trying to accomplish it. But, Judge...I can't figure out *why*. Why do you do it? You give so much so freely," Peter required longingly, "I need to know, Judge, it's been pestering me ever since the thought entered my brain, and I just don't know."

The Judge smiled and seemed to have become overwhelmed. He stood up and walked over to the window, still not saying a word.

Peter was fixated on the Judge, awaiting in suspense the Judge's response.

He finally spoke, "Peter, I have devoted my whole heart and soul to this Town in the best way that I know how. I have given all there is I believe *to* give from my heart and soul," he said with a crackly voice, paused, then continued again, "I know every person in this Town. I have been where many of them have been. I have been, *them*. Peter, I have *been* you." He turned to look Peter in the eye.

This struck Peter.

"Peter...you are particularly special."

Peter was enthralled with what the Judge was telling him and wanted to know how or why he saw him this way.

"You are, *different*. Exceptional, but distinctive and unique." The Judge contemplated for a moment, "Peter, this Town is a body, an entity, a *being*; and *you* are the heart and the mind. You've witnessed the division within, now Peter, *you* need to be the good. *Be good*," the Judge spoke firmly, but with care.

Peter felt it.

Several weeks later on a beautiful day, Peter, after walking around the quieter parts of the Town for some time, found a bench in an area that had many trees and people that blew around the walking paths like the leaves of the trees. One such leaf blew onto his shoe, it caught his eye, and he picked it up and began studying its intricacies, marveling at the subtle beauty that can be found—that is almost hidden sometimes, or forgotten—in the simple things, which we take for granted in life. A middle-aged woman walked by with a bright colored purse, winning Peter's attention, he was brought back to watching the people as they drifted by. He wondered what made them tick, what was inside them, what their lives consisted of— good or bad, where they were going. Just then, James walked up. "Hey, Pete! How you doing?"

"James! The man, the myth, the legend! I'm doing swell, how are you, my friend?"

"I'm doing good, buddy. Doin' good," answered James. He then gave an awkward glance at Peter's companion sitting beside him, not knowing how to address it, "I, uh, I see you still have that dog hanging around you, eh?" he asked uncomfortably.

Peter looked at the white dog and back at James, smiled and said, "Oh yeah, this is my *new* dog friend. His name is Rein."

THE END